INVISIBLE
FENCES

Norman Prentiss

This special signed
edition is limited to
750 numbered copies.

This is number __431__

INVISIBLE
FENCES

Invisible Fences

Norman Prentiss

CEMETERY DANCE PUBLICATIONS

Baltimore
❖ **2010** ❖

Cemetery Dance Publications
132-B Industry Lane, Unit #7
Forest Hill, MD 21050
http://www.cemeterydance.com

First Limited Edition Printing

ISBN-10:   1-58767-184-0
ISBN-13: 978-1-58767-184-5

Cover Artwork © 2010 by Steve Gilberts
Interior Artwork © 2010 by Keith Minnion
Interior Design by Kathryn Freeman

For my Father and Mother,
the first storytellers of my childhood—

For my brother—

And, especially, for Jim.

Special thanks to: early readers Michael McBride, Mark Sieber, Boyd White, Susan Taylor, and Douglas Clegg; Steve Gilberts and Keith Minnion for their amazing artwork; Gary A. Braunbeck, Kealan Patrick Burke, Rich Dansky, Ed Gorman, Joe Howe, Tim Lebbon, Thomas F. Monteleone, James Newman, David Niall Wilson, and T. M. Wright, for their kind words; Brian and Kate Freeman; Mindy Jarusek; Andrea Wilson; and Rich Chizmar, who sent a very brief, very welcome e-mail.

PART ONE

THERE'S an invention for today's dog owners called an invisible fence. It's basically a radio signal around the perimeter of the yard, and if the dog steps too close to the signal, it triggers a device in the animal's collar and delivers a small electrical shock. Perfect Pavlov conditioning, just like I learned back in ninth grade psychology class. But it seems a bit cruel to me. The dog's bound to be zapped a few times before it catches on. Dogs aren't always as quick as we are. Hell, growing up we had a mongrel lab that would probably never have figured it out: Atlas would have barked at air, then -zap!-. Another bark and charge then -zap!- again. I loved that sweet, dumb animal.

Still, I guess for most dogs the gadget would work eventually. Inflict a little pain and terror at the start, and then you're forever spared the eyesore of a chain-link fence around your front lawn.

"THE BIG STREET"

WHEN I was growing up, my parents invented their own kind of invisible fence for me and my sister. All parents build some version of this fence—never talk to strangers, keep close to home after sundown, that kind of thing. But my parents had a gift with words and storytelling that zapped those lessons into my young mind with a special permanence.

My father taught Shop—excuse me, Industrial Arts—at Kensington High School, so I guess that's where he built up his skills with the cautionary tale: don't feed your hand into the disc sander, keep your un-goggled eyes away from the jigsaw blade, and other Greatest Hits. But listen to his rendition of that old stand-by, "The Big Street":

He walked me and my sister Pam to the divided road on the north end of our community. I was six, and Pam was three years older. He stopped us at the curb of McNeil Road, just close enough where we could hear the cars zip by, feel the hot wind of exhaust or maybe get hit by a stray speck of gravel tossed up by a rear wheel. A half-mile down, on the other side of McNeil, was a small shopping center: a single screen movie theater, Safeway grocery, People's Drugs, and a Dairy Queen, among other highlights. In the other direction visible from the top of this hill was Strathmore Park, with swings, monkey bars, and a fiberglass spider with bent-ladder legs. We could visit these wondrous places anytime Dad drove us there, but we were never, ever, to cross the Big Street on our own.

"Now, let me tell you about a boy who used to live the other side of the road," our father said. "About your age, Nathan. He crossed back and forth over this Big Street all the time." Dad swung his arm in front of him, parallel to the road. "Looks like a pretty good view of the road in both directions, doesn't it?"

We both craned our necks and followed the swing of his arm. Pam nodded first, and I did the same.

"Well, you'd be wrong. Some of those cars come up faster than you think." As if to confirm his point, a blue truck rattled past. "When you do something a lot, you get pretty confident. Over-confident. This boy, he'd run across early that morning without a hitch, like usual. On his way back, he was standing right where we are now. Looked both ways, I imagine, or maybe he forgot that one time—we don't know for sure. What we *do* know..."

Dad dropped to one knee, the toe of his right sneaker perfectly aligned with the edge of the curb.

"See right there, where the gutter doesn't quite match the road? Not too close, now, Nathan." He stretched his arm out like a guard-rail, and I leaned against it to peer over. The blacktop of the road had a rounded edge, about an inch higher than the cement gutter, but the asphalt was cracked or split in a few places. One spot, it looked almost like somebody'd taken a bite out of it. I guessed that was where Dad wanted me to look.

"His foot likely got caught in that niche, and the boy tripped into the road. The black van might have been speeding, might not. But it wasn't entirely the driver's fault, was it?"

I swallowed hard, my throat dry. I'd have loved a Misty or a dip cone from Dairy Queen, but I sure didn't plan on crossing the Big Street to get it.

"See that dark patch in the road?"

I leaned forward again, and my T-shirt felt sweaty where my chest pressed against Dad's outstretched arm.

"County trucks cleaned things up, best they could, but you can't always wash away every trace of blood."

A shadowy stain appeared beneath the rumbled flashes of painted steel, chrome, glass, and rubber tires, a stain wet and blacker than the gray-black asphalt, in which I could almost distinguish the outline of a boy, just my size.

• • •

"I'd heard the story before," Pam told me that afternoon. We had separate bedrooms in our small house on Bel Pre Court—a luxury a lot of our friends didn't enjoy—but I was in and out of my sister's room all the time. She even let me use the bottom shelf of her bookcase to store a few Matchbox cars, a robot, and a plastic astronaut.

"Really? Did you know the kid who got hit?"

"No, I heard it before from *Dad*. Two years ago."

Pam had fanned baseball cards in front of her on the bedspread. She'd invented this game of solitaire: traded players, constructed her own all-star teams, grouped them in batting orders, then shuffled the cards to start again. Often she waited long minutes between each shift of card, as if the game required intense, chess-like concentration. She never could quite explain the rules to me, but I didn't mind: I wasn't that keen on sports like Pam was, and I was happy she still managed to talk with me while she played.

"The kid wouldn't need to cross the road," Pam said.

"Huh?"

"All the good stuff's already on his side. Movie theater, playground, burgers and ice cream. Why cross?"

I hadn't thought about that. "Maybe he had friends over here."

"Nope. The friends would all be visiting his side, where the fun stuff is. They'd be the ones who got whacked by the *black van*."

She said "black van" in a sing-song voice. I didn't understand why she'd make a joke, go so far as to imagine more kids killed while crossing McNeil Road.

"I saw the stain on the road," I said.

Pam switched two baseball cards, then flipped another one face down. "Probably a car broke down on the side of the road, leaked a little oil. Check our own driveway, and you'll find a few stains there, too."

"Not like that stain," I said.

"Okay."

"He showed us where it happened, Pam."

"Okay."

Pam had pretty much destroyed our father's story with logic. She was three years older, obviously a little more worldly than I was. But I don't think I was naive to side with my Dad. More than logic, it was the *story* that convinced me. The confirming details of the cracks in the asphalt, the boy-shaped stain on the road, summer's heat and the rushing cars making me dizzy—just like must have happened to the careless young pedestrian in Dad's account. Maybe it wasn't true, okay, but it could be true if somebody didn't follow the rules. Accidents happen. We may not all have friends who've chopped off a digit or two with the buzz-saw in Industrial Arts class, but if a couple circles of red marker on the shop tile, scrubbed into faded realism after hours, help the teacher point the next day and shout, "There! There's where the fingers rolled off and bounced like link sausages onto the floor!"—well, strictly true or not, such lessons are worth learning.

No way was I going to cross the Big Street on my own.

"Dope Fiends"

THE next summer, Mom staked a claim to her own span of our invisible fence. Dad came up with most of the stories, so in retrospect I'm grudgingly proud of Mom for thinking this one up.

A deep stretch of woods formed a natural barrier behind our house. Dad had a few gems about kids getting lost, bitten by snakes, or swollen and itchy from a patch of poison ivy—all of which generally kept us from setting up camp in there. We wandered into the woods sometimes, peeling bark off trees, flipping logs to look for ants or pill bugs, poking a stick at a rock to make sure it's not a bullfrog. As long as we didn't go near Stillwater Creek, we didn't get in trouble. The creek had its own persuasive power: it was muddy, shallow, and stank of sulfur, so Pam and I steered clear without being prompted.

But Mom, overcautious, decided we shouldn't venture into the woods at *all*. One rainy day, she called us into the living room where she typically sprawled out on the sofa and watched her "plays" on CBS. "Turn down the television, would you? I've got something serious to talk with you kids about."

With the rain outside, and the shades pulled down, the living room was pretty dark. The main light source was the television, which reflected a kind of campfire glow on Mom's face as she talked. "There are dope fiends in the woods," she told us. "I heard about them from Mrs. Lieberman."

• • •

I have to explain a few things about my Mom before I go any further.

When I was three years old, my baby sister was born. I remember playing with her, in particular a game where Pam and I lined up plastic bowling pins around the rim of Jamie's crib. She'd wait for us to finish, then knock them over with her tiny fists, and laugh and laugh. That's mostly what I remember, the laughing.

Jamie had to go to the hospital when she was about fourteen months old, after a really bad cough developed into something more serious. Apparently they put her in a croup tent, a plastic covering that kept away germs and allowed doctors to regulate her oxygen. I never visited her in the hospital, but my parents later told me how much Jamie hated that tent. I imagined her beating at the plastic covering with her fists, but too weak to laugh or even breathe.

I don't remember what my parents said the last night they returned from the hospital. I know they must have agonized over how they'd break the news to us, my Dad no doubt holding back his natural tendency towards the grisly, giving us the soft version of Jamie drifting painlessly off to sleep and never waking up; how babies were innocent and always went to heaven, so she's with God now, and we'll always have our memories; Mom convincing us that *we're* all right, that *we'd* never get that sick, and Mommy and Daddy would always be there to protect us, and nobody's dying, not anytime soon that's for sure, we promise; and all the time both of them trying not to cry themselves, knowing if they messed this moment up it could haunt me or Pam for the rest of our lives.

I know they worked really hard on what to say, and I'm sad I don't remember any of it. But I was only four, and memory keeps its own protective agenda for a child that age. Just the bowling pins, and the laughter.

There's a Polaroid of me and Pam taken the day of Jamie's funeral. Pam's in a frilly peach dress, holding a small bouquet of daffodils. I'm wearing a tan suit—a handsome little gentleman, in a heart-breakingly tiny clip-on tie. We're standing next to the grave marker, which has a hole in the center where Pam will soon place the daffodils. According to my father, before Pam had the chance to fit the stems into the grave marker, I kneeled down to peer deeply into the hole. "Jamie's down there," I said, then waved. "Hi, Jamie!"

• • •

But I was talking about my mother.

After Jamie's death, not right away, but gradually, my Mom became more and more withdrawn. She didn't have a job, and never learned to drive, but she used to go shopping with my father, or went with us on day trips to visit relatives in Silver Spring or Tacoma Park. She also maintained a small garden out front, and played bridge twice a week with neighboring housewives. After the tragedy, she told Dad she didn't feel like talking with family about Jamie, not for a while at least, and somehow that ended her drives to the grocery store, as well. The bridge games slipped to once a week, and then just the gardening. And then not even that.

Agoraphobia roughly translates to "fear of open spaces," but that's not exactly right. It's a kind of depression that, in my mother's case, at least, was more about avoiding interaction with other people. Dad and Pam and I were the notable exceptions. She didn't want to see anyone

else, and she didn't want anybody else looking in—which explained why she lowered the living room shades, even during the middle of the day. Eventually she refused to leave the house for any reason—certainly not for the psychiatrist visits that probably would have helped her, if people hadn't frowned so much on therapy in those days, or if my Dad had been strong enough to force her into treatment. His version of "strong" was letting her have her way, adding cooking and cleaning to his breadwinning duties, with Mom on occasional assist with the child care when absolutely necessary.

But more often than not, it was us kids doing things for her. Mom spent most of her time on that sofa, to the point that it's hard for me to recall her in motion. Certainly she must have moved from the bedroom to the living room on occasion, definitely needed to use the bathroom like the rest of us. But mostly things were brought to her: a cup of water with ice and a bendable straw; Diet Rite Cola in the tall glass bottle; two peanut butter and banana sandwiches for lunch, the crust removed; and a small plate of Oreo cookies with a mug of milk for her afternoon snack. She had a remote for the television, but mostly watched the soaps and local news on channel 9, and if either Pam or I were passing nearby when she wanted to switch, she'd have us turn the channel.

Mom's other entertainment was newspapers, with a special fondness for the crossword puzzle and the Word Jumble. She stored the day's puzzle folded over like a napkin on her TV tray, next to a plate of food, and worked during the commercials or during an especially slow-moving plot on *As the World Turns* or *The Edge of Night*. Some days she didn't finish the puzzles, or didn't skim her way through the rest of the newspaper sections. Stacks of newspaper piled next to her beside the sofa, beneath the TV tray, and at her feet. Mom could never keep straight which stack was the most current, so when Pam asked for today's Sports page or I wanted to read the comics, we each had to choose a pile to sort through.

Dad taught summer courses. Even between terms he went to school on a nine-to-four schedule, and used their shop equipment for woodworking projects he solicited via purple, mimeographed ads stapled to telephone poles throughout our neighborhood. All for the extra money, of course, but just as likely because the day-dark house bothered him in ways it wouldn't bother little kids who didn't know much better.

At least, not usually. But that overcast, rainy day when Mom told us about the dope fiends, the bleak, shadowy living room gave her words the chilly certainty of a midnight-whispered campfire ghost story.

• • •

"The police found needles in the woods," Mom said. We stood next to the couch and

Mom sat up, a striking change from her usual horizontal posture. "Just thrown on the ground where kids like you could step on them in your bare feet. They found rubber tubing, also. These dope fiends tie tubes around their arm to make the veins stand out, then use the needles to inject drugs into their bloodstream." She lifted her crossword-puzzle pencil and mimed jabbing it into her forearm.

Due to my twice-yearly doctor visits, I was already plenty scared of needles. I never escaped without some vaccination or another—for German measles, smallpox, tetanus, whatever. After losing Jamie, Mom wasn't taking chances with me or Pam. I hated the awful tension when the nurse squirted a faint arc of fluid over the sink before she plunged the stinging needle beneath my rolled-up sleeve. The needle was too long and thin; I worried it could snap off inside my arm and hurt forever.

The idea of tying a tube around your arm sounded complex and painful to me. Who would do something like this on purpose?

Fiends, of course. A much better word than "addict" for kids. The word addict scares adults, because it's all about loss of control—our fears that we'd drink or gamble or screw against logic, throw money we don't have into greedily programmed machines or wake up late mornings with a monstrous hangover and an even more monstrous bedroom companion. Kids don't fear addiction (they don't have much control

over anything to begin with). Better for them
to visualize some tangible bogeyman, like the
monster *under* the bed or evil trolls who live
beneath storybook bridges.

"I know you kids would never be foolish
enough to try drugs," my mother continued.
"But if you run across a group of dope fiends,
they may force their drugs on you. Chase you
down, and whoosh!" She jabbed her pencil in the
air towards Pam for emphasis, then towards me;
I jumped back in nervous reaction.

"The police haven't caught any of the
dope fiends yet, so they're still out there." She
pointed at her main sources of information:
the television, in its rare moment of flickering
silence; disorganized towers of newsprint; and
the end table telephone, her daily link in epic
half-hour conversations with her two remaining
friends, Mrs. Lieberman and my Aunt Lora. "If I
hear anything more, I'll let you know. Until then,
I want you both to stay out of those woods."

I nodded first, without waiting to see Pam's
response.

This was before a president's wife told us to
"Just Say 'No'," before "Your Brain" sizzled
sunny-side-up in an MTV frying pan. But even
then, in the post-hippie 1970s, drugs were dialed
pretty high on a kid's panic-meter. I was too
young to grasp the concept fully, of course, and
stirred my own fears into the mixture. When my
mother mentioned the "paraphernalia" found in
the woods—hypodermic syringes, rubber tubes,

empty glass vials of medicine—she may have said something about medicine caps. Or maybe the "dope" idea was suggestive enough. My third grade mind somehow latched onto caps, conflated it with the image of a cartoon child in the corner of a schoolroom, a pointed dunce or dope cap rising from his head. I imagined predatory older boys donning these caps as the proud symbol of their gang. They patrolled the woods behind our house, seeking new initiates—would toss syringes like darts at your exposed arms or neck, then would force you to the ground and press their ignorance into you, lowering it like a shameful cap onto your struggling head.

Ignorance was even more terrifying to me than needles. I was a slightly overweight boy, uncoordinated at sports and generally unpopular at school. To be stupid—to be unattractive and awkward and picked-on *and* stupid—was the worst fate I could imagine. Smart was all I had.

• • •

And yet I was stupid enough, later that summer, to let Aaron Lieberman and my sister talk me into visiting those woods to search for abandoned needles.

SUNDAY MORNING

THE agonizing stretch between 10 a.m and noon every Sunday morning was without doubt the most mind-numbingly boring interval of my childhood.

Dad preferred not to go to church alone. With Mom's stubborn agoraphobia, that left me and Pam as potential company. Neither of us liked church: the wooden pews were uncomfortable, and the monotonous Catholic mass lacked for us the religious significance our father so evidently derived from it. Worst of all, the final service of the day was a 12:15 "folk mass" at Saint Catherine's, that church's desperate attempt at "hip"—as if bad singing and silly acoustic guitar arrangements were enough to spark young people's faith. The folk mass was the one Pam and I usually got stuck with, if we ended up going at all.

Here was the odd thing about Dad and church: he wouldn't drag us out of bed and make us go. I guess he thought we should practice religion willingly, or it wouldn't be meaningful. If we were up and around, though, he'd ask us to get ready for the next scheduled mass, and in that trapped interchange, neither Pam nor I would have the heart to say we'd rather stay home. The only sure church-avoidance strategy, which Pam and I developed independently and practiced with varying success, was to make yourself sleep past noon.

Seemed easy enough. We'd stay up as late as we could on Saturday night, watching horror movies introduced by Count Gore de Vol on Channel 20, or switching to Ghost Host with the snowy reception of Baltimore's Channel 45. No matter if the creature feature lacked a creature—like that Japanese mushroom-people flick with no Godzilla to stomp the cast into oblivion, or the "old house" mysteries from the 40s where foolish people ran from room to ghost-less room. Sometimes the films portioned out a few decent scares between the "Hair Club for Men" commercials, enough to distract us while we waited for the night to become our own. We watched television in the den, on the other side of the kitchen from Mom's living room. During the first feature, Mom disappeared to join Dad in their bedroom (did we ever see her go? At some point we'd look past the kitchen doorway to the other end of the house, her couch empty against the far wall). To extend the night past Ghost Host's nonsensical farewell ("Here's blood in your eye!"), we'd play a game of Life, steering blue- and pink-pin families in plastic cars over plastic hills or, even better, Monopoly—the full version, not the quick cheats with dealt-out properties or "Free Parking" windfalls. The longer we stayed up, the easier it would be to sleep late on Sunday morning.

In theory. I could usually drowse past the departure time for the 10 a.m. mass, easy, but eventually I'd hear Dad fixing himself breakfast in the kitchen, the murmur of Sunday news programs from the living room. With a hopeful stretch I'd grab my metal-band watch from its place around the bedpost, certain it was nearly noon, and see the phosphorous hour hand aimed squarely between the ones in eleven. No matter how hard I tried, I couldn't get back to sleep: I'd toss and turn, check the watch again, distinguish a few stray words or commercial jingles from Mom's TV, rearrange my pillow, check the watch again (only 11:15!), and, defeated, resign myself to a hard wooden seat and the latest strummed arrangement of "The Lord's Prayer."

Seems silly now, all that effort. Church itself couldn't be any more tedious than those endless minutes of feigned sleep. But even in summer, when every day was free of school and schedule, I still fought to avoid that single hour in church.

Maybe it was a competition with Pam (who "won" more mornings than I could count, Dad and I leaving for church without her). Maybe it was an early instance of childhood rebellion, a passive battle against a father I loved but subconsciously blamed for my mother's infirmity. Whatever the case, those hard-won mornings where I did sleep long enough were sweet victories. The day was mine: a quick slip into fresh underwear and yesterday's shirt and blue jeans, and I'd escape into noon-day sun with the whole world open to my explorations.

Within the accepted boundaries, of course.

• • •

Atlas had wrapped his rope around the tree in our front lawn again. He panted against the trunk, collar stretched tight and his water bowl temptingly out of reach.

"Retard," I said, and the dog barked in agreement. I pointed to his left, made a "go 'round!" motion with my hand, but all he did was twist his head, brown ears flopping stupidly.

"C'mon, boy. I'll show you." I walked counter-clockwise around the tree, and Atlas followed me. If I stopped, Atlas would have stopped too, not grasping the concept of the wrapped leash. I had to go all the way around for each of the six twists.

The ground remained spongy beneath my feet. Dad had tied Atlas's leash to the porch banister, since the wooden spike wouldn't stand firm in the lawn. We'd had a week of off-and-on heavy storms, thunder and loud downpours that rattled like gravel tossed against the windows and aluminum siding. Mom watched the televised weather reports from the safety of her sofa. "You wouldn't catch me outside in that mess," she said more than once.

July 18, 1971. That Sunday morning's victory over church and time and weather was cause for a special celebration—maybe even a little mischief.

I heard the screen door screech open and bang shut. "Wasn't sure I'd make it this morning," Pam said, then she bounced down the three cement steps. "I had to fold one end of the pillow over my eyes to block the sunlight."

She picked up a gray tennis ball, muddy and matted with dog drool. "Ready, dummy?" She moved the ball back and forth; Atlas followed the motion, as if shaking his head in the negative. "How about now?" This time, with Pam moving the ball up and down, Atlas nodded "yes."

No matter how dumb the dog, you can teach it a trick or two. You just have to figure out the right kinds of tricks.

"Here," Pam said, and she tossed the tennis ball straight up into the leafy oak. Atlas stood under the tree and barked as the ball bounced slowly down, ricocheting from limb to limb. It took an unexpected hop before the last drop, but Atlas caught the ball in his mouth after the second soggy bounce.

"Your turn," Pam told me.

I didn't much care for this next part. Atlas was a gentle dog, not at all intimidating. He wouldn't give up a toy easily, though. Pam and Dad both liked to grab a ball or rag or bone in Atlas's mouth and try to pry it free, tugging and making fake growling noises to taunt answering growls from Atlas—deep yet playful, almost a parody of canine anger. His lips snarled up over the gums, yellow teeth gleaming large and slick. Atlas was a big dumb dog, but he was Atlas, so I wasn't scared he'd bite me. But big dumb dog mouths produce a lot of drool: I didn't want that smelly, slimy stuff on my hands.

Pam was watching, though, so I went through the motions. I pinched the ball between the tips of my finger and thumb, tried to tease it out gently, but Atlas nudged his wet nose into my palm then shook his head back and forth, slobbering on the inside of my hand. With my other hand, I tried to pinch his jaw at the hinge; Atlas opened his mouth, the ball shifted, then Atlas clamped down on it again. I tried a tighter grip on the ball, my pinky rubbing against the dog's slimy tongue, and I felt the jaw start to slacken. The instant I pulled the tennis ball free, Atlas let loose a head-shaking, lawn-sprinkler-style sneeze.

"Yuck," I said while Pam laughed. "You can have your nasty tennis ball." I dropped the ball at the dog's feet, then held my right hand away from my body and shook it in the warm air.

"Hope you don't catch Atlas's cold," Pam said. Funny thing: neither of us tended to get sick in the summer, but we suffered more than a few fever-less headaches or stomach cramps during the school year. Mom was sympathetic to any illness, and didn't question us if we somehow healed miraculously once the school bus pulled away from our street. Still, some of Mom's germ phobia rubbed off on me, especially when I thought of a dog's bad breath heating up its thick, sticky drool. Not bad enough for me to run inside and wash my hands with soap and water, you understand, but enough to make me feel icky for a little while.

"Let's see who else is around," I said. We liked to do a sweep of the back yards in our neighborhood—better than calling people on the phone or knocking at their doors, since you could see right away who was around, and if the other kids were having any fun. If you just drop in on a group, it's easier to leave if you get bored.

The Liebermans, directly across from us in the cul-de-sac, was a popular stop. They had a decent play set in their back yard, with two swings and a slide. There was a fun element of danger to these swings: if you arced out too high in front, the whole metal frame would lean after you a bit, its rear legs lifting slightly out of the ground. They'd thump back in place as you swung back, a satisfying rhythmic drumbeat over the squeal of metal chains. Lots of fun, as long as Aaron's sixth-grade brother wasn't around: he was a swing-hog, and rude on top of that, adding a "y" to the end of mine and Pam's names to emphasize how much older he was compared to us. "Hey, Natey and Pammy," he'd say, "you here to pway with widdle Aaron?" I couldn't figure out how him talking like a baby was supposed to make *us* look childish, but it seemed to work that way.

That afternoon, their back yard was empty. I could see why: the ladder-and-slide end of the play set hovered a foot over the lawn; the swing-seat on the furthest side lay on the ground, its chain hanging slack.

The rain must have softened their ground even more than ours. Pam started laughing.

"What?" I said. We had visiting rights for this play set. As far as I was concerned, this was a tragedy.

Pam stopped laughing long enough to explain. "Big shot David must have been in for a shock when he sat his fat butt in that swing!"

And I caught Pam's joke. David pushing his brother aside in a race to the swings this sunny morning, heaving himself into the seat, and then the whole side of the play set sinking to the ground beneath him. If that wasn't exactly what happened, that was how I wanted to picture it.

"What's so funny?"

My face flushed at the high-pitched voice, and I turned expecting to see David's rude expression. Instead, it was Aaron, his natural voice closer to his brother's mocking lilt than I'd previously realized. Aaron had quietly opened their kitchen's sliding glass door and regarded us from the Lieberman's cement porch. He held a half-eaten strawberry Pop Tart, and wore the same green shorts and blue-striped shirt he favored for summer months. He was an okay kid, but he tended to dress in seasons: the winter outfit was brown corduroy trousers and an orange wool sweater; spring brought out the blue jeans and a button-down denim shirt; the autumn collection was tan corduroy and a red lumberjack-flannel shirt. I thought maybe he had identical pairs of the same clothes, but one winter Monday he tore a hole in the right knee of his corduroy pants. It grew slightly larger in the same place each passing day, until the knee was covered by a patch on Friday.

Of course, kids my age didn't always pursue things to their proper origins: Aaron's wardrobe was more a sign of his parents' (in those pre-liberated days, his Mom's) laziness, not bothering to dress the kid nicely until he'd reached the age when such things mattered (whenever that was). Or maybe a sign the family wasn't as well-off financially as their fancy backyard play set would indicate, and they'd cut corners with the clothes and laundry budget. I never actively teased Aaron about his wardrobe, which is some comfort to me now, but I remember having the vague impression my friend was like a cartoon character, Charlie Brown in every single panel with the same shirt, black mountain-peak stripes across his chest.

"Nothing's funny," Pam said. "What happened to the swing set?"

"Storm damage," Aaron said.

"Like what? Struck by lightning?"

"Something like that."

I couldn't look at Pam, but thought I heard her stifle a snort.

"You guys want a piece of toast?" Aaron asked, indicating his Pop Tart.

"Sure," I said, and we followed him into the Lieberman kitchen.

• • •

The quick snack was fairly uneventful, but I ate gratefully, hungrier than I'd realized. The older brother stepped into the kitchen at one point to grab a can of root beer from the fridge, but fortunately David left without making a snide comment.

Aaron collected our napkins and empty milk glasses when we were finished; he shook the crumbs over the sink, then turned on the faucet to rinse the glasses. I only half paid attention, but he seemed to be standing in front of the running water longer than he needed to, his elbows lifted on each side in an odd stretching motion.

As Aaron returned slowly to the square kitchen table, he held both hands behind his back. Aaron veered toward the side of the table where I was sitting, then he lifted his right arm level with my head, fingers curled toward the ground. In one quick motion, he squeezed his thumb forward to meet his fingers.

A thin crystal arced from his hand. An ice-cold whip lashed my face and neck and I jumped back, nearly knocking the chair over as I stumbled from the table.

Cool water ran beneath the collar of my T-shirt.

Aaron smiled, and turned his hand over.

"Oh my God," Pam shouted. "Where'd you get that?"

In his upturned palm: a hypodermic syringe.

● ● ●

"I don't want my Mom to hear."

Aaron should have considered that before he squirted my neck with ice-cold water. He was lucky I didn't shout loud enough to bring the whole neighborhood running.

"Let's go back outside." Aaron used both hands to pull open the sliding glass door, then stepped onto the patio. We joined him, but nobody spoke until after Pam closed the door behind us with a heavy click.

Pam stepped forward with her hand out. "Let me see it."

"Sure," Aaron said. He traced a little path in the air with the syringe, treating it like a toy airplane. He made a buzzing noise then veered it in a mock crash landing towards Pam's hand. She didn't flinch, and I figured out why: the nose of the "plane" was flat, with no needle at the tip of the syringe.

Pam pulled out the plunger half-way, then pushed it back in with a faint hiss of air.

Thin black lines and small numbers marked the clear plastic casing. The syringe was thinner than I expected, about the diameter of a pencil.

Then Pam pulled back the plunger again, and twisted her face into a goofy wide-eyed expression. She placed the syringe above the bend in her left forearm, then pressed down hard enough that I saw her skin dimple beneath the tip.

"Don't, Pam," I said.

She drove the plunger home with her thumb, then screwed up her face in a farce of agony and bliss. I looked away.

Aaron was smiling. "Cool."

The next few minutes, Aaron used the garden hose to show us how to fill the syringe with water. Instead of pouring a thin stream of water through a hole, as you did with a normal squirt pistol, the trick was to put the tip of the syringe in the stream and pull back the plunger. Water dragged in after the retreating rubber plug, filling the cylinder like magic. I was the last one to try it, and the simple motion made the syringe less threatening. That, and its relative ineffectiveness as a squirt gun. You only got one shot, and the aim was unpredictable—a dot of metal remained in the plastic tip where the needle had been broken off, misdirecting the arc of water.

I took a "revenge" shot at Aaron, and mostly missed. Maybe a little on his sleeve.

"We should put cherry Kool-Aid in this thing," Pam said.

"Blood, huh?" Aaron pondered the idea as he took the syringe back from me. I wasn't sorry to give it up, but I was glad the syringe had lost some of its power to frighten me.

"Yeah," Pam said. "You could jab it in your arm, then scream like you messed up. Blood everywhere!"

Great. And now I wondered about the missing metal point—if, as my mind sometimes pictured it, the needle had broken off in somebody's arm, a metal splinter tearing along a vein, the blood flow's force pushing it further inside, tumbling like a whisk through fat and muscle tissue until it reached the heart. With each heartbeat, the lodged needle would scratch at the chest from the inside—an endless, painful metronome.

Or something like that.

Pam looked at Aaron. "Where'd you find it?"

"Where do you think?"

"Any other needles? Could you take us there?"

He shrugged, answered a single "maybe" to both questions.

Pam's eyes lit up.

"But what about..." I had to speak. "What about the dope fiends?"

Even as I said the words, rich with all the haunting connotations conjured up in the dark of our mother's living room, the phrase sounded foolish. Fiends, in our quiet suburban neighborhood? Proof stared us in the face, a hypodermic syringe apparently used to initiate a crazed drug binge. And yet, Aaron had tamed that horrible icon, needle broken off the tip and the stupefying drugs chased from the plastic cylinder with cleansing streams of water. An unspoken childhood dare hovered over us, as well: Aaron, the small boy whose mother also warned of dangers in our woods, had ventured into that wilderness and returned unharmed.

One additional comment about Sunday mornings: my Catholic upbringing designated this as a "day of rest," which might be another reason why Dad chose not to wake us for church. It was intended as a thoughtful, reflective day, a religious day. But for me and Pam, when our ploy to oversleep succeeded, the sweet freedom made it more of a stolen day. We'd tricked Dad—maybe even tricked God in the process—and that gave us some extra license. If we were ever to break a rule, Sunday was the day.

And so...

THE WOODS

MY left tennis shoe squelched in mud, and I almost lost my balance. The woods had suffered the same week of heavy rain as the rest of the neighborhood, and now the dense trees overhead kept the sun from drying the ground.

"Maybe...over here." Aaron was supposed to be leading the way, but he had a tendency to drop back slightly. Pam overtook him a few times, then stopped and glanced over her shoulder for Aaron's guidance.

It was hard to tell where we were headed. We'd passed our usual area at the perimeter, with its familiar landmarks: the double-trunk tree that split like a wishbone; the heavy boulder Pam always tried, unsuccessfully, to roll; the pile of abandoned lumber, too rotten to inspire dreams to build a secret clubhouse. Now we traveled strange ground, doing our best to locate naturally formed paths that wove between trees.

Enough sunlight filtered through leaves to help us see, but it seemed darker the further along we got. The air smelled of dust, humid and misting along my exposed arms and legs, prompting sticky sweat along my shirt collar and behind the bends of my knees. The throbbing buzz of insects seemed to thicken the air as well, adding to my confusion.

"That tree looks familiar," Aaron said. The tree he pointed to had no distinguishing features at all. He might as well have said "eenie, meanie, miney, moe" to choose our next turn.

I checked my watch. 1:15, which meant we'd been in the woods about ten minutes. Time to worry not about where we were headed, but how we'd find our way back. I'd have to trust Pam's sense of direction; I couldn't keep the twists and turns straight in my mind.

I tried for a heavier tread, to press more obvious footprints into the muddy ground—an improvised version of Hansel and Gretel's breadcrumbs. "How much farther?"

"Close," Aaron said. "I'm pretty sure."

He'd said the same thing two minutes ago.

Eventually, a sulfurous smell wafted into the hot mist. A faint murmur mingled with the steady thrum of insects.

"Did you go as far as the creek?" Pam asked.

• • •

The murmur got louder with each step, the only obvious path forcing us down a slick slope toward the rising smell. I wanted to cover my nose, but needed to keep my arms out for balance.

"You don't know where we're going," I said to Aaron. "I don't think you've even been here before."

"Maybe to the other side of…that tree." He pointed at another identical oak or maple or whatever. Pam charged ahead, her momentum fueled by the path's downward slant. I paused every few steps to secure my footing, which made it hard for me to keep up.

Careful as I was, I slipped and fell next to a puddle. My hand sunk into stagnant water, and a mush of brown clay oozed between my fingers.

My face flushed, and I prepared myself for the laughter and scornful pointing that usually greeted one of my pratfalls. Instead, I heard only the rumble of the nearby creek. The path in front of me was empty.

I got up, then with quick steps and slides I followed the curve of the slope.

Pam and Aaron stood motionless after a sharp bend in the path. But they weren't waiting for me to catch up.

They were looking at the creek.

Today, more like a river.

THE LOG BRIDGE

PAM and I had always avoided the creek, so we didn't have an obvious point of comparison. Even so, recent rains had clearly caused the creek to rise higher than it should have.

About a dozen feet ahead of us, creamy brown water rushed past, the roiling surface flecked with swirls of heavy tan foam. Although fresh rain should have diluted the creek's tell-tale odor, the extra motion seemed to have unearthed new offenses, stirred them and mixed them and carried them foully through the air.

Instead of the muddy, pebbled banks you'd expect beside a creek, the waters reached to a line of trees on either side, and weaved among slightly submerged trunks.

It was as if a river had dropped here out of nowhere. I couldn't trace the original creek path beneath it.

Most amazing of all, the constant rain had weakened the foundation of a large tree; its roots and trunk had split from the bank and the entire tree had fallen on its side. It now formed a perilous bridge over the rushing water.

"No," Aaron finally admitted. "I've never been here before."

I remember thinking about the log bridge in *King Kong*. The ship's crew ran from a man-eating dinosaur, rushed over a fallen log, only to have their escape blocked by a giant, angry ape. Kong lifted the trunk from his side, and shook the men off the log one by one. They each fell screaming into the pit below.

Practically in our back yard. A lost world.

"Oh my God," Pam said, her voice pitched to a shout over the roar of water. "What happened to *you?*"

She'd turned around and was pointing. Aaron turned as well. Against the wondrous backdrop of foamy dark water and fallen tree, they stood and pointed and laughed.

I looked down at my shirt, ridiculously splattered along the front. My right hand wore a brown glove of mud, with long chocolate smears on my shorts where I must have wiped off the excess.

"Did you crap yourself?" Aaron asked.

"I fell."

"Uh, no kidding." Pam snorted, more than she had at her earlier vision of David's humiliating swing-set disaster.

In an instant, the magic of the moment was gone. I wasn't on some movie set or in a storybook fantasy land. I was where kids often ended up: in an embarrassing situation, with no exit to slink through.

Did we ever miss an opportunity to be cruel? Even with siblings, especially with friends?

Let me tell you about friends. I didn't have many. Aaron was my best friend by default—proximity in the neighborhood, his Mom friends with my Mom, and at school we suffered a fairly similar level of peer tyranny. I was the third geekiest kid in our grade level; Aaron was second. How did I know this? Well, whenever Aaron was absent from school, I got picked on twice as much by the other kids. The two of us, together, sometimes picked on Ralph Fancy, our grade's number one geek (and yes, his last name was part, but far from all, of Ralph's problem).

Now, as Aaron joined my sister in booming laughs at my misfortune, I hated them both a little bit. But I hated the predicament more, my clothes soiled and the rancid odor of the risen creek asserting itself anew.

"Where'd you find the syringe?" That would get him. I knew he didn't have an answer.

"Nowhere," Aaron said. "I get allergy shots each month, and the nurse sometimes breaks off the needle and gives it to me." His voice, loud over the rushing water, expressed a kind of confidence he'd never had before. "I just wanted to see how far you guys would go."

I was ready to run at him, head butt him in the stomach and knock him into the brackish water. See how funny *that* was. Pam, I knew, would be furious about the wild goose chase.

But she laughed again, not bothered at all. "Doesn't matter." Pam waved an arm over the water. "Look what else we discovered!"

Two against one. I was supposed to play the role of "good sport," no matter how much I wanted to rush home and ditch these uncomfortable, mud-soaked clothes. No choice but to stay, really. I didn't know my way back through the woods.

"Let's look at the tree stump," Pam said. She used other trunks to support her, staying a few feet from the water's edge as she walked to the fallen tree. Pam didn't look back to see if we followed her. I let Aaron go first.

The trunk was gigantic—half again as tall as Pam. Its gnarled roots stretched in several directions like the tentacles of a desperate octopus.

"I wonder what sound it made when it fell," Aaron said.

Pam smiled. "No sound, since we weren't here to listen."

On one side, the roots dipped below the surface of the water. The rushing creek splashed loudly against the trunk and the clumps of disturbed earth. A Pepsi can rattled against the side, and a cardboard carton had hooked strangely on an extended root, just above the water line.

"Hand me that branch," Pam said, her feet anchored against the dry edge of the trunk.

Aaron figured out where she pointed and grabbed at the long overhanging branch on a nearby tree. He tried to snap it, but the wood wasn't brittle enough. He had to bend it back and forth, then tear it from the tree like it was a drumstick torn from a roasted chicken.

"Here you go." Keeping his distance, he passed the branch to my sister.

Her feet steady against the trunk, her right hand tight around a thick root, Pam extended the branch past her left arm and poked at the trapped carton. Her first few movements misjudged the distance, but she finally caught one of the side flaps with the stick and lifted.

Aaron leaned forward, but only slightly. Like me, he was too timid to approach the water's edge.

We couldn't quite see inside. Pam tried again with the stick, this time lifting up a second flap then pushing the entire box away from the root. The box floated back, caught a spin in the current, then ducked under the tree and sailed out of sight down the creek.

Nothing. In the movies, a severed head might have fallen out, or at least a dead animal.

"This is stupid," I said.

"No, it's not." Aaron maintained an undeserved pride in the scene. Sure, he'd led us here—but by accident. And now he was letting Pam do all the dangerous work.

"I dare you to walk across," I said to him.

• • •

Well, why not? The fallen tree really did span the risen creek. Maybe these woods were like our neighborhood: all the good stuff on the other side of a Big Street we weren't allowed to cross. Maybe we really would find abandoned needles on the other side of the creek. Or something better: an empty clubhouse; a bird's nest of speckled eggs; a thick, rubber-banded stack of dollar bills we could split three ways.

The tree would be wide enough to walk on for the first part of the crossing, a fairly straightforward balancing act. Further across, as the branches and leaves sprouted in different directions, it would be a simple enough task to find your footing. Just like climbing a tree, except you'd be climbing across, which was better than the increasing threat from gravity if you climbed straight up.

I dare you.

But he wouldn't. Aaron would be too chicken to make the attempt, and that would end it. Humiliated, he'd agree this was stupid, and we should head back home.

"Worth a try," he said. Before I could stop him, he slid down near Pam and reached for the dry roots on the right side of the trunk. The roots were spaced almost like a ladder, and he stretched an arm toward one high over his head.

And: "Faked you out!" he said. He spun around laughing. "No way I was gonna do—"

Then it was Aaron's turn to slip and fall.

• • •

It was almost comical, the look on his face. He'd spun around to laugh at me, and one foot just kept moving. His leg went sideways, like he'd swung at a football and missed. Then his body did a little ballet wiggle: his arms grasped in the air at roots that weren't where he expected them, then he twisted back and the ground wasn't where he expected either, then water was, beneath him, his body caught in a strong current that was ready to pull him away.

(Now you might understand the significance of the box from earlier. We needed to see the empty box spin its perilous path along the rushing current. That set up the suspense—established the danger Aaron was in now, if he followed that same path out of sight.)

Like Aaron before the splash, the moment itself twisted in the air, suspended between tragedy and comedy. I imagine my younger self with muddy hands raised over my mouth, either to stifle a gasp or hide a smirk. What saved the moment—and Aaron, of course—what made it okay to smile and maybe point and laugh and think, "You got what you deserved for fooling around, for fooling us," was...

For all its rushing force, the creek wasn't really that deep.

Aaron wasn't swept away by the current; he didn't sink beneath the surface, a trail of bubbles leading to a murky unknown depth. Instead, he stood there in the creek, a few feet to the right of the fallen tree, about six feet from the raised bank where Pam and I watched him. Aaron's arms and head remained safely above the water line, five of his shirt's horizontal blue stripes clearly visible. His hair wasn't even wet.

He swayed for a few seconds as the water foamed past him. He balled his hands into fists. The spray misted the lowest of his visible stripes into a rich, dark blue.

Then he started to walk. His elbows winged out to each side, his fists nearly touching in front of his chest, Aaron swung his shoulders back and forth. If we could see beneath the water, we could have watched him lift his legs, knees high and feet lunging forward.

But he made no progress. He was like one of those stupid mimes, doing the standard "walk in a windstorm" routine.

Pam yelled out to him. "Are you stuck?"

"No," Aaron said. "The water's too strong in front of me." His voice cracked with a tremor of anger and humiliation and fear. "And the ground's slippery."

He stopped moving and looked around for a minute, as if he could read an answer in the ripples of the water, in the gnarled bark of the fallen tree. "I could try moving sideways, I guess. If I reached the tree, I could pull myself along."

More swinging of the arms and shoulders, but Aaron was still a mime in a windstorm.

He stopped, and looked at us.

"You might still be able to swim," Pam said. "If you push yourself forward with enough force..."

Aaron nodded his head back and forth, his lips tight.

Pam had moved closer to where Aaron had fallen in. She tucked the toe of her left foot beneath a sturdy root, and leaned forward. Her torso swung out over the water and she stretched out her arm, but her reach was too short by about three feet.

"Nathan, maybe if I hold your arm real tight, you can wade into the water and pull him in."

I wished Pam hadn't spoken so loudly. Aaron heard her, brightened up a bit, said "Yeah, Nathan!" and waited for me to dive in. Two against one, again.

My earlier pratfall was still on my mind, the slime of mud and puddle water damp on my skin and my shirt and the seat of my pants. The creek water was far worse: loud and stinking of filth and whatever awful decay the recent rains had unearthed and stirred into a foul broth.

"Swim," I said. "Why don't you swim?"

Aaron knew how to swim. The Liebermans, in addition to their backyard swing-set, owned summer memberships to the municipal pool, and took yearly vacations to Ocean City.

With Dad's summer school job and woodworking projects, he'd never taken us to the pool. We'd gone there a few times with our cousins, but always stayed in the shallow end. I hated getting wet—even there, with water that was clear and smelled only of bleach and the vague threat of other children's pee. A couple times I breathed water up my nose by mistake, which led to fits of gasping coughs, and bleachy soreness at the back of my throat. It surprised and outraged me that my nose and throat were connected: smell and taste were different senses, after all.

"Just push yourself forward," I told Aaron. I stayed back a few feet from the water's edge. "We can grab you from here."

Then Aaron started getting mad. He waved his arms and screamed at me. "This is serious, Nathan!" The language he used next, if I transcribed it here exactly, would not have the proper effect: we were elementary-school kids in the seventies, in the years before cable television brought "fuck" and "shit" and "asshole" into everybody's homes. "Retard" or "homo" or "pussy" were about the best we could manage, but those childhood insults no longer parse. "Poohead," historically accurate, provokes a giggle; I need the anachronistic shock of something like "motherfucker."

Not simply to convey Aaron's rage—which was considerable, his hands scooping the surface of the creek and splashing rancid water toward us. But to convey how it felt to me, to be called these names by my friend. Not in the joking way friends spoke sometimes, not even how your enemies might taunt you in the hallway between classes. Aaron threw these ridiculous names at me, and he meant them.

Still, I refused to wade into the creek. His shouts and stirrings made the water all the more unappealing, and I stepped a little behind Pam to keep out of splashing distance. I could hear the names he called me, though.

That's when I solved the problem.

I picked up the branch Pam had used to dislodge the cardboard box. It was about three feet long, probably enough to extend her reach to Aaron.

"Use this," I said, and handed it to Pam. The branch had been too stubborn to snap when Aaron tried earlier to break it off the tree. It would be just as sturdy as a rope.

Pam poked the stick forward, just as she'd prodded earlier at the cardboard box. She had the advantage this time of using her right arm, so her aim was better. She slapped the end of it at the water next to Aaron, then held it steady for him to grab.

Which he did. His right hand caught it, then he heaved his left hand and shoulder over. That branch was all he needed: Aaron moved now with an effortless grace, making his previous helpless flailings all the more ridiculous in comparison. A few simple hand over hand motions and he'd pulled his whole torso out of the water. Two steps now, legs high and feet lunging like I'd imagined them earlier, and he made it to the ledge.

Aaron sat cross-legged on the ground, his arms in front and curling into the mud as if afraid he'd slide back into the water. Even over the steady rumble of the creek, I could hear his heavy, gasping breaths.

I held out my hand to help him up.

He raised his head, his mouth a thin line and breaths coming loud through his nose. He pushed my hand away, and stood.

"I could have drowned," he said, a calm steady voice that gained strength as he continued. His voice had a raspy quality that sounded less like my friend and more like his older brother. I stepped back from him, edging closer to Pam, beside her, then putting her between us as he invoked the names again, the curses and insults of a child, then a new insult, "coward," with the added threat that he wanted to kill me.

I turned and ran back through the woods.

• • •

Three sets of footprints marked the path, making it fairly easy for me to retrace my steps away from the creek. I scrambled up the muddy slope, steering wide of the puddle where I'd fallen on the way down. Even in my haste, I sought solid footholds: dry patches of ground, or buried rocks or tree roots that jutted from slick mud.

When I'd nearly reached the top of the slope, I heard footsteps behind me, splashes and heavy wet slaps of someone taking less care to study the ground as it rolled beneath. I imagined Aaron closing the distance between us, his anger urging him up the slope. He'd dive at my legs to tackle me, climb onto my back and push my face into warm, swampy ground.

Any other time, I wouldn't have run from Aaron. We were the same height, but my chubby build gave me the advantage over his thin, gangly body. If we'd ever had cause to fight, I'd have won. Of course, I never expected we'd have reason to come to blows, and my surprise at his anger, at the venom in the words he'd spoken earlier, gave the situation a nightmare quality—as if my friend had been transformed into a rabid animal.

I worried that panic would cloud my judgment, send me blindly down the wrong fork in the path, one early mistake compounded by each subsequent turn to twist me further and further into unfamiliar territory. The path ahead looked different in reverse; the ground was smeared in both directions, no clear sign which way we'd traveled earlier. I took the fork on the left.

Perhaps I'd chosen this route simply because it seemed brighter and easier to follow. Shadows from overhanging limbs hatched the dirt, and I hurried from one lighted island of ground to the next. Still, my pursuer edged closer. I heard the slide and slush of sneakers through mud, a quicker pace than mine and accompanied by forceful exhalations of breath I could practically feel on the back of my neck.

I turned to face my pursuer.

Pam.

"Keep going," she said as she caught up alongside me. Her left hand reached out to rest on my shoulder, urging me forward. "This way," she said next, and steered me into a nearly hidden path between two trees. A low hanging branch brushed along the top of my head. I didn't remember ducking beneath this branch when we'd approached from the other side, but I trusted Pam's sense of direction. Whatever happened, at least we'd still be together.

Then, under the comfort of Pam's guidance, I decided to worry about Aaron. I didn't want him to catch us, obviously, but I also didn't want to abandon him to wander the woods all alone.

"Aaron won't get lost, will he?"

Pam stopped and leaned against a tree, surprised I'd care what happened to my friend after the way he'd spoken to me back at the creek. She waited a moment, closed her eyes and tilted her head to help her listen, then squinted at the path. She pointed the way we'd come. "He's right behind us," she said.

I saw him in the distance. Aaron's clothes were so covered with mud they blended into the green and brown like a military camouflage uniform. He was bent over slightly, hands on his knees as he paused to catch his breath.

Initially, Aaron's proximity prompted us to move faster through the woods. As our track grew more twisted and confused, however, I continued to worry that he'd lose his way.

"Where is he?"

"He's right behind us," Pam repeated.

And he was. Aaron kept a deliberate distance. When Pam and I got tired and slowed down, Aaron slowed as well. If he caught up, he'd have to follow through on his threats and the two of us would get into a fight we'd later regret. If we kept our distance now, in a day or two we'd be back to normal. From my experience, childhood friends never stayed mad at each other for very long.

Eventually we reached the pile of abandoned lumber, then the unmovable boulder. Aaron could thread his way through these familiar landmarks—no need for us to glance over our shoulders to see where he'd paused with heavy breaths at the latest turn in the path. We sprinted ahead, burst out of the woods, then raced over safely mowed suburban grass toward home.

HOME

ATLAS yapped as we turned the corner into our front yard. I had hoped to get into the house quietly, sneak past Mom who may have fallen asleep on her living room sofa, and change into fresh clothes before she saw me. "Quiet, retard," I said, but Atlas stood next to an overturned water bowl and continued to bark. Pam kicked the tennis ball toward him, which distracted him for a moment.

Our mother kept the house locked at all times, as if we lived in what newscasters called a "high crime area." Flecks of dried mud fell like scabs from my hand as I reached into my pocket for the house key. I opened the screen slowly then eased the key into the knob, twisted, then pushed in the door.

"Nathan? Come here."

We barely had time to shut the door behind us before she'd called out. From the living room, Mom couldn't see which of us had stepped inside, but she often asked for me specifically. My sister was more independent, more likely to respond "Just a second," then need to be prompted again five minutes later.

Pam slid past me to the hallway that led to our bedrooms. I wiped my feet quickly on the foyer mat, brushed at the front of my shorts and headed into the living room.

The afternoon was still sunny, but the closed shades and curtain might be enough to mask the stains on my clothing and smudges on my hands, knees, and face. If I was lucky, Mom wouldn't look at me at all: she often kept her eyes on the television screen while she talked to me or Pam.

"Where you kids been?"

"Nowhere. Goofing around with Aaron."

"You weren't at their house." Not really a question: obviously she'd spoken with Mrs. Lieberman on the phone while we were out.

"No. Their swing set got broken from the rain." I kept my right hand, the muddiest one, behind my back. She turned her attention to me for a moment, but seemed to stare only at my face instead of at my clothing. A commercial for Promise margarine played in the background. Brightness flickered from the screen, and I imagined waves of color tracking over me like spotlights in a prison yard.

"Make me a sandwich," she said.

"Okay. I have to use the bathroom first."

"Wash your hands when you're done," she yelled after me.

THE SWINGS

IT was a while before I gathered up the nerve to visit Aaron. That, and I actually managed to catch a rare summer cold—provoked, no doubt, by the teeming cocktail of germs and smells of the creek. For a few days, Pam had the dubious honor of caring for me and Mom at the same time.

I headed over alone, approaching the Lieberman's back yard with cautious steps. The play set had been repaired, and Aaron sat on the furthest swing. His legs hovered over the ground, and his arms grasped the chains on either side. His older brother stood next to him near the support post.

When he saw me, David walked quickly in front of Aaron and blocked me from approaching. "What do you think you're doing here?" he said.

"I wanted to talk to—"

"You little shit." David drew closer, a tight fist raised near his chest. He was about a head taller than me, thin like his brother, but with an unpredictable anger that added an air of menace. "You could have helped him."

"I did," I said. It had been my idea to use the stick to pull him out—though obviously Aaron's version of events had emphasized my cowardice.

"You left him there," David said.

"No. He was right behind us. We went slow, so he could follow us out of the woods." I kept looking around David's body, past his raised fist, at Aaron. My friend sat sullenly in the swing and stared at the ground. He wouldn't even look at me.

"Tell him the truth, Aaron," I said. And David hit me.

I'd always been scared of getting into a fight, of getting beat up by larger, older kids. Now, the blows that landed on my shoulder and my chest weren't as painful as I'd feared. But the idea of getting hit still frightened me, and I cried out.

Loud enough that Pam came running. Somehow I'd ended up on the ground, curled into a ball with my hands over my head. David punched at my back a few times before Pam stepped between us.

She was closer to David's age, closer to his size, but he didn't try to fight with her. It was still taboo for a guy to hit a girl, even if she was a tomboy.

"Come on, Nathan," Pam said, and motioned me ahead of her toward home.

I picked myself off the ground. When I glanced back briefly, David held his arms straight against each side, fists clenched. Aaron looked up finally, his face blank and accusing.

• • •

Aaron never spoke to me again. The way he managed to represent the story to his family, I had masterminded the visit into the woods. I'd dared him to climb on the log bridge (true, as I've already admitted). I'd refused to help him from the water after he fell in the creek, then ran out of the woods with my sister—abandoning Aaron deep in the maze-like paths.

He'd arrived home covered with mud, and he turned me into an enemy to escape his punishment. No blame for my sister, the eldest and most responsible in our group: I was the friend, and should have looked after Aaron more carefully. Aaron's parents ordered him to stay away from me.

Me. Weak, uncoordinated, overweight. The third nerdiest kid in our grade at school. Somehow I'd become a "dangerous influence."

Don't go near that evil, scheming, friend-deserting Nathan, or...-zap!-

I'd become part of another kid's invisible fence.

• • •

Mom's friendship with Mrs. Lieberman didn't last much longer. They had a few phone conversations, but only five minutes each, compared to their usual half-hour gossip sessions. Mom barely spoke during these calls: just a few interjected agreements while Mrs. Lieberman's voice buzzed from the phone's tiny speaker in an angry monotone.

The summer just didn't feel right anymore, and I wasn't looking forward to going back to school. No doubt Aaron's mother had spread the news about me to parents of other kids my age. The "bad-boy" reputation wouldn't match my physical appearance, and I'd just come across as a jerk, a laughing stock. I'd knock Ralph Fancy out of his number one spot, and that geeky kid would be making fun of *me* soon enough.

So I wasn't terribly upset when Dad announced the family was moving at the end of August to Alabama. He knew a school principal in Graysonville, and could get a job as a Special Education teacher. Dad also told me and Pam that he needed a drastic change from the house in Maryland: "Too much of your mother's papers here, and she won't let me throw anything away. If some of it gets lost in the move, well, that can't be helped."

A good story, like a lot of Dad's stories. But I always thought the move was because of me.

PART TWO:
CAUTION

A Promise

LIKE most people's superstitions, mine are selective and irrational. I don't believe in any form of good luck: rabbit's feet, lucky numbers, rubbing the belly of a Buddha statue. Superstitions about bad luck, however, have more emotional truth for me. I'll avoid black cats and the underside of ladders, and will pinch spilled salt and throw it over my shoulder.

Because the one time I crossed my Mom's warnings and wandered deep into the woods behind our house, it turned out my best friend would never speak to me again.

As an adult, I follow most rules to the letter. Not because I respect the rules, necessarily, but because the one time, the one time I edge over the speed limit or underreport my taxes or leave a door unlocked for five minutes, I believe that something terrible will happen.

Consider which of these scenarios is more likely: 1) someone wins a contest the first time he enters; or, 2) the winner, jumping for joy with his lucky ticket, drops dead of a heart attack. My luck, I'd be the second guy.

Terrible things may still happen to me, but I won't seek them out. No bungee-jumping or skydiving for me. I am not the leather faced eighty-six-year-old woman who dares cancer by smoking two packs every day of her long life. Neither am I the wild partier whose slowed, overcompensating reflexes somehow swerve past deserved late-night collisions.

I'd rather be overly cautious.

I want to coast into my tragedies.

• • •

All this to explain why my life might sound rather dull.

I've stayed in Alabama since we moved here in the early seventies. Pam and I went to a poorly funded elementary school, followed the same small groups of kids through junior high to high school. Pam left Alabama after she graduated, but I went to a small state-run college. After that, I took a job with the local library branch, housed in a former post office, and I've worked almost twenty years in the same position.

Forty-two years old, and I've never been in a romantic relationship. I'm fairly average-looking, almost like the movie stereotype of the spinster librarian. Except, of course, I'm a guy. I don't know if that makes me a sadder case or not.

Most years, the biggest excitement in my life is when the "theft detector" goes off. Bookmobiles in other states have a better selection than Graysonville Public Library has in its catalog, but we still have a decent security system: not much stuff, but we want to keep it. I'd planted metal stickers in each book myself, small magnetized strips hidden in the binding or beneath the card holder or in the crease between two pages. Libraries have used this technology for years—an early version of the invisible fence designed for dog collars.

People have this "zapped" look on their faces when the warning buzzer goes off, and it's easy to tell that they're shocked. They're not professional thieves—just absent-minded. Most often, it's adults who forget to check out their books before passing through the security gates. Kids usually remember.

• • •

Pam had strained against the confines of small town life. She was wild in high school, smoking with friends on the front steps between classes, parking with boys in the lot behind the Fruit of the Loom factory on weekends. As soon as she turned eighteen, she left for a job with a New York software firm. We talked on the phone now and then, but not in much depth. Five years ago, I was surprised to learn she'd broken up with a live-in girlfriend.

Myself, I grew to appreciate the small town calm, and things seemed to get easier each year. Once you were fixed in people's minds as the librarian, as the "confirmed bachelor," they pretty much left you alone.

Except, of course, for Dad, who wanted grandchildren. I was closer, so I bore the brunt of his teasing and cajoling. I was also the "go to" person in case of any emergency, and was expected to visit Mom on weekends while my father immersed himself in woodworking projects. "You're not doing anything else," Dad would say. "You don't have a date, do you?"

• • •

Sometimes I thought of my parents as a burden. A continual source of bad luck, perhaps, like a gypsy curse. Other children feel this way too, I know, so it's not a particular source of guilt for me.

It's difficult to express how strange it was to grow up in their home. First, for all Dad's remarks about needing a drastic change from our Maryland home, the house on Jackson Lane was uncannily similar. It was a single-floor building, since my mother refused to go up and down stairs. The L-shaped layout was the main change, but otherwise it had the same number of rooms. The furniture from the Maryland house followed us, and took its place in roughly equivalent positions. After only a few weeks, my mother had accumulated enough newspapers to reproduce the familiar towers around her living room couch. The same dark green curtains hung over the windows, shutting out light and protecting her from imagined mobs of prying eyes.

For me, it was as if the new house in Alabama was haunted by the house in Maryland. My mother, especially, added to this impression. I don't have many memories of the move itself, but I imagine her packed into the dark cab of the moving van, riding the 800-mile distance lying on her couch and facing an unplugged television, at ease amid the crowded stacks of inanimate objects. Over the years, my mother aged like a piece of furniture: instead of wrinkles, her skin warped or cracked like a badly varnished surface; her pallor went from indoor white to a muted gray, as if she were covered by a thin layer of dust. She was a voice from the darkness, a controlling presence that projected from the living room into every corner of the house.

Even when I visited my parents as an adult, familiar objects from my childhood, shifting piles of junk and strange plays of light and dark, and my mother's voice through it all, combined to give their home a haunted atmosphere.

• • •

I'd mentioned how Pam and I, as children, stayed up late each Saturday night in an attempt to sleep through Dad's visit to church the next day. As I'd pointed out, we watched a lot of late-night television, with particular scorn for the "fake" horror movies: ones that didn't show the monster, or haunted house stories that turned out not to have any real ghosts.

When I speak about Mom and Dad's house on Jackson Lane as haunted, and it's only a metaphor, that's the kind of cheap literary device that really angered me and Pam as kids.

Be patient.

Before it's over this story will, I promise, summon up a real ghost.

Likes and Dislikes

How's Mom?" I could tell Pam didn't want to ask the question, but she knew why I'd called.

"The same. Fever of 102, and trouble breathing."

Pam sighed. "She should be in a hospital."

"I agree."

"You should make her go."

"Easy for you to say. You're not here."

"Okay, then. Dad should make her go."

"They're stubborn. Mom cries and wants to stay home. I tell Dad she won't get better on her own, and he says he has to 'respect her wishes'."

"He's always done a little too much of that. He should dial 911 and let them decide."

"I think he's embarrassed about the house. The paramedics would need to clear a path through all the junk."

"God, I can't even picture it." Pam hadn't been to the house in almost ten years, but I'd given her a pretty good idea of the condition. The main change was due to the Home Shopping Channel and Mom's convenient couch-side telephone. I think some of the operators at HSC knew her by name. She had more electronic gadgets and kitchen appliances than anybody in Graysonville, some still in the UPS boxes they'd been shipped in. And Joan Rivers jewelry—ones where you could snap out the glass "jewels" to match the colors of different outfits (many of *those* still pinned in flat, laminated rectangles, never to be worn).

"I'll come down if you think I could help," Pam said.

"Come down if you want to see them."

"Yeah, maybe I will. I'll probably call Dad, see what he thinks."

"Good idea."

Dad would never invite her down. He'd say not to worry, Mom was getting better.

Then she'd get worse, then it'd be too late, and then Pam would *have* to visit.

• • •

When I was twelve, Aunt Lora stayed with us for a week. Dad cleared out the guest room, basically by moving everything into the garage. Lora was technically my Dad's sister, but she'd been my Mom's closest school friend since the eighth grade, so I tended to think of her more as from my mother's side of the family. Aunt Lora had an amazing obsession with neatness, so it was fun to see her navigate our home. In addition to the guest room, she cleaned the kitchen, the hall bathroom, and the area around the living room chair closest to Mom's couch. Each of these clean spots were her sanctuary against encroaching clutter—but to her credit, she never complained about the house, and cheerfully sat with my mother for extended in-person versions of their daily phone sessions, and running commentaries on *As the World Turns* or *Love is a Many Splendored Thing.*

She also cooked for us, which was a tremendous change from peanut butter sandwiches and Dad's package-mix dinners. The thing I complimented Aunt Lora most on, though, was a lemon layer-cake she'd made from scratch. At the time, I'd thought there were only two kinds of cake—chocolate and "regular," with corresponding brown or butter-cream frosting. I liked the cake partly from novelty, but the novelty wore off when Dad made his own version of lemon cake for each of my subsequent birthdays. At one point I tried to tell him I needed a change, and he gave me an incredulous look: "You *love* lemon cake."

He never let me grow out of my childhood likes and dislikes. Perhaps if I did something he recognized as "adult"—move out of state like Pam, join the Army, maybe, or get married and pop out the grandkids he wanted—maybe then I'd be allowed to change. But I did change, in more subtle ways than he was able to notice:

The simple pleasure I got from my low-paying library job ("Are you ever going to get promoted?"). My book collecting hobby, with a special weakness for Victorian novels in three-volume editions ("Can't you get a paperback for cheaper? It's the same book!"). And my modest apartment, large enough for me, one cat, and a lot of Dad's bookcases ("If you had a house, I could build you a dining room table and chairs." Or, less subtle: "I built a wooden crib for the Fergusons. Too bad you don't need one.")

Mom noticed, though. She kept the windows closed tight, but studied the world through her television screen. In the seventies she laughed at the gross innuendo of *Three's Company* and *Match Game '75;* she picked up street slang from *Miami Vice* and other cop shows in the eighties; and developed an edgier sense of humor as the nineties brought sitcoms like *Friends* and *Seinfeld.* Dad worked in the real world, while Mom lived through MTV's version. Ironically, the woman who was afraid to step outside her house had smoother, more adaptable social skills.

In her last years, I grew to enjoy my weekend visits with Mom. In addition, I'd often call at

night to check in—usually after 10:00, once my father was already asleep. We'd talk about what was on TV, what movie I'd gone to see, who'd checked what book out of the library. Back in Maryland, it was my fault Mrs. Lieberman stopped talking to her on the phone. I'd like to think I made up for it, eventually.

One night we were talking over the late night news. I heard the local CBS anchorman in the background—Shane or Marv, or Frank-something. And she just said: "You're happy with your life." It wasn't phrased as a question—just a simple observation, not even prompted by anything we'd said before.

I could honestly answer, "Yeah, I am."

• • •

After Dad retired in '92, Pam and I would sometimes indulge in morbid speculations about which of our parents would die first. It wasn't exactly a game of choosing your favorite, but had more to do with practical matters.

—Who was healthiest? They'd both developed diabetes in their old age, but Mom tended to cheat by eating real candy, including *the largest Hershey bar I'd ever seen! Ten pounds, Pam. I don't know—I guess she ordered it off the TV.* Obviously our father got more exercise. *But Nathan, Dad's more likely to get in a car accident or fall down an elevator shaft.*

—Who had the stronger will to live? A tough one. After retirement, we worried Dad would go stir crazy. Instead, he found more woodworking projects, did substitute teaching, and played poker and bridge games three times a week. *But Mom's got her "plays." God forbid she never find out if Laura recovers from amnesia or if Allison's twin sister fools the Addison family out of the inheritance.*

—Which of them would be hardest for us to care for? No question, Mom. She was okay during the day, but needed Dad to do everything once he got home: cooking, shopping, laundry, other essential cleaning. Dad was self-sufficient, but Mom would need full-time care. *And what's this "us" business, Pam? We know you don't have room in your tiny New York apartment. I'll be stuck with whichever one survives.*

—Who would be the best company? I had my answer, but Pam insisted Dad would be less bother. *You always liked him better. You went shopping with him and bought comic books at Drug Fair; interned with him two summers at Pelham Elementary. And those goofy stories which you loved: car crashes and poison ivy and sawed-off fingers. He was your lifeline, Nate.* True. But our childhood likes and dislikes can change.

Mom finally ended up in the hospital. I called the ambulance myself, while Dad waved his arms and threatened to disconnect the phone.

FIRST

HE dressed Mom in one of the nightgowns she'd ordered from the Home Shopping Network, a cheerful floral pattern that struggled to offset the weak, dusty blue pallor of her face. Dad insisted we flank her on each side and practically carry her to the front door before the paramedics arrived. She wasn't as heavy as I expected—but then, she hadn't eaten much over the past few days.

Turned out her flu symptoms had developed into double pneumonia. On top of that, she had an irregular heartbeat—possibly congestive heart failure.

How strange it was to see her in a brightly-lit hospital room. A frail elderly man occupied the bed closest to the window (Dad's insurance policy only allowed for a semi-private room);

the man kept the curtains drawn aside and the blinds open. Different nurses hustled in and out during my visit, and Mom seemed not to mind the attention.

I visited each of the four days she was in the hospital. If Dad was there, he'd go to the cafeteria for coffee or a snack, to give me time alone with her.

The day she died, she still had a clear plastic mask over her mouth and nose, with oxygen tubes to help her breathe. She had to move the mask aside anytime she wanted to speak.

I did most of the talking. I even switched TV channels for her, like Pam and I used to do in the old days. She'd nod and hold up a weak hand when I reached a program she liked.

After a while, I sat next to her quietly. She drifted in and out, her eyelids heavy. Then both her hands moved slowly to the plastic mask, and I turned the volume down on the television and leaned closer to her face. I could hear the strain of the elastic bands, the scrape of plastic against skin as she slid the mask aside.

"I'm sorry," she said.

"What for?" I responded. "You don't have anything to be sorry for." And I patted her hand and kissed her forehead.

• • •

Pam came down for the funeral, of course, and Aunt Lora as well. Most of the Graysonville attendees were from Dad's school, or his group of card players. A little under twenty people in all. A respectable-sized crowd, I guess.

We'd had a bit of confusion about the viewing. Initially it was to be closed-casket, since Mom was such a private person most of her life. Then Dad saw the job the morticians had done, and he thought she looked good. "Leave it open," he said, which made me a little angry. I sat with Aunt Lora for most of the two-hour viewing period.

"Your mother was smart," she told me and Pam. "I used to check my homework against hers, and she was always right. And she knew electronics. When I needed to hook up my VCR, I called her and she talked me through it better than the damn customer service at Best Buy. That picture is crooked." Aunt Lora leapt up from her seat after this last comment and crossed the viewing room to a framed landscape print. She nudged the bottom right edge of the frame to make the picture even with the hatched pattern of the funeral home wallpaper.

Pam and I looked at each other and tried not to bust out laughing.

• • •

"You know, I promised myself I'd never step foot in here again."

"I figured as much."

Pam bent down and scraped her finished cigarette against the edge of the concrete porch. I hadn't let her smoke in my car on the way from the funeral parlor.

She'd emailed a few pictures, but it was strange to see her in person. Her hair was shorter than she'd worn it as a kid, but still thick, her natural curl matted with gel into shiny waves. The style seemed old-fashioned, almost business-like, to match her charcoal jacket over a blue open-collar shirt.

It was easier to talk with her on the phone. No awkward pauses, unsure where to direct my eyes.

"Where's...?" My voice trailed off.

"Sondra. I asked her not to come." She took a deep breath, exhaled loudly. "Let's get this over with."

"Sure." I pulled out a separate key ring with a tiny LED flashlight attached (a free gift after some over-$50 Home Shopping Club purchase). Turned out I didn't need the key: behind the screen door, the front door was unlocked. That never would have happened while Mom was alive.

I stepped into the foyer and held the edge of the door for Pam. She paused at the entrance, then put her head down and pushed forward. Her body trembled as she passed the threshold.

Then, nothing.

Pam was struck by it too, I could tell. The hollow atmosphere of a house that, for twenty years, had never for a single moment been empty.

I didn't want to leave the hallway, step into that awful, cluttered, uninhabited living room.

"She would have called one of our names by now," Pam said eventually.

"Yeah."

Our own voices seemed to break the spell. I led the way; my feet had worn a familiar path along the foyer tile and into the flattened green-and-mustard shag carpet.

The heavy curtains were pulled aside from the windows, shades lifted. Dust, surprised by sunlight, hovered like drunken gnats. Nothing had been cleaned or removed, but some of the newspaper stacks had been dragged away from the front of the couch and lined up against the wall. Several UPS boxes, pushed to the front of the room, covered the television screen.

The couch seemed untouched. Two cotton towels lay over the sofa's ridged fabric, which Mom had declared as too scratchy to be comfortable against her bare legs and arms. A memory of our mother's shape left a depressed outline in the cushions beneath the towels.

"Dad always blamed this clutter on her," Pam said. "We'll see how long it takes him to clean things up."

Mom's phone was still perched on the end of her rickety TV tray, with several outdated issues of *TV Guide* next to it. A yellow recipe card box held pens, pencils and Post-It notepads. A newspaper section was folded back on the Jumble page, circles filled in for three of the four words.

"Look at this," I said. Beneath the table were two small cartons made of rugged black plastic. They were snapped shut at the handle, like toy briefcases. Mom had written my name on a sticky-note attached to the top case, Pam's name attached to the other.

I handed Pam her case and lifted the plastic clasp on mine. It was some ridiculous thing called a "LightDriver": a flashlight with a tool-attachment node on the opposite handle. Snapped into compartments on the inside of the case were three rows of tiny screwdriver and wrench attachments. Even with my limited knowledge of tools, I could tell the design was flawed. The flashlight would shine in your face instead of on the worksite while you tried to use the screwdriver at the other end. Peggy on Home Shopping would say how great it was to have all these tools in one convenient place, the "Items Sold" counter would click higher and higher, phones ringing off the hook in the background, and most people would think, "What idiot would waste money on something like that?"

I started to cry, and when I looked at Pam she was crying too.

• • •

We were there because Dad had asked us to stop by the house. He'd uncovered some of Pam's things—"Maybe worth something on eBay"—

and gathered them in a box in her old bedroom (now better known as junk storage room #3).

As reluctant as Pam was to revisit our parents' home, it gave us a chance to get away from the funeral crowd. After the viewing, there was a reception at the house of one of Dad's card-playing buddies. We were expected to attend, but could use the house visit as a stalling tactic.

Pam walked down the hallway, carrying her tiny "LightDriver" briefcase at her side—a comic addition to her business-like attire. I followed her into her room on the left.

There was barely space for both of us inside the doorway. Pam's twin bed was still in the far corner, pointed away from the window, but it was impossible to reach it. Boxes covered the bed, some with paperback books, others with vinyl albums and cassette tapes. Examples of my father's handiwork covered the floor space— wooden shelves, dressers, and oversized storage chests shoved tightly together in an abandoned spatial puzzle.

Pam's box was balanced on the edge of an open-top wooden crate filled with kitchen appliances (including a toaster-oven, an old-style coffee percolator, and two waffle irons).

"Oh, these will make me a fortune," Pam said. She reached down and pulled out a shoebox, the bottom of it stained with water damage. Inside were her baseball cards. The ones on top were too worn to interest any serious collector; further down in the box, the cards were warped, stuck together, and coated with mildew.

Also in Pam's box were a few of my things from the Maryland house: matchbox cars (rusted), and my plastic robot and bendable Major Matt Mason spaceman.

"What a bunch of crap," she said. She tugged at a red corner of fabric tucked deep in the box, then pulled out and unfolded a wrinkled felt pennant for the Washington Senators. Pam had rooted for the team for a few years after we moved out of Maryland, but then the D.C. owner sold the ball club to Texas. She tossed the pennant and shoebox back into the larger box.

A gold-painted frame was flush with the back side, picture facing the cardboard. "Don't tell me..." Pam lifted it, and turned the portrait around. "I can't believe he put Jesus in here."

It was a "floating head" picture, Jesus with eyes slightly upturned, his face surrounded by a shimmer of light. In my youngest years, it hung in Mom and Dad's bedroom. At the end of each day Pam and I were called in to sit on the edge of their bed, fingers interwoven and facing the picture for our nightly prayers.

"I wondered whatever happened to this guy," I said.

"I think after Jamie died, Mom took it down." Pam slid the picture back in the box, the frame askew and one Jesus eye peering over the top of the shoebox.

"Remember the 'glow'?" Pam asked, miming quotation marks in the air with hooked fingers.

I shook my head.

"You were pretty young. Dad used to tell us if we did an extra special job of saying our prayers, the picture would glow. You know: a sign of Christ's approval."

I didn't fully remember, but as Pam spoke I caught the texture of a wish, a child's wonder.

"You asked me once if I saw the glow," Pam said. "I could tell you tried pretty hard for it: saying the prayer in the right order, concentrating on each word, remembering at the end to bless our relatives and neighbors and the babysitter. You looked disappointed, so I told you it was just Dad's trick to help us pray better. That pissed you off—at me, not at Dad. You always believed Dad's stories."

I thought then of my younger self, four or five years old, striving for some sign of approval from a dime store painting in a gilded frame. Would the halo shine like neon? Would Christ's entire face brighten, light stretching away like lines from a cartoon sun, heating the painted frame into red-hot metal? None of it happened.

"I was pretty gullible, I guess."

"Maybe," Pam said. "He let Mom die, you know." The comment seemed to come out of nowhere. I wouldn't normally expect Pam to stand up for our mother. Of the two of our parents, Mom did the most to push Pam away. Every weekend night of my sister's high school years, Mom yelled at Pam from the couch: she insisted Pam abide by an unreasonable 10 p.m. curfew, then screamed criticisms at her the instant she pushed in the front door after midnight.

"Blame me, too," I said. "We should have taken her to a hospital sooner."

"I'm not talking about now," Pam said. "All those years, ever since Jamie died. When Mom wouldn't leave the house. Dad was letting her die. It just took a while."

As Pam spoke, her words felt like the truth.

SOON, MAYBE

A commonplace about long-married couples was that once one of them died, the other would soon follow. There was a morbid undertone to Pam's "See you soon, maybe," when I dropped her off at Birmingham Airport after Mom's funeral.

Actually, Dad seemed to bounce back easier than I expected. He added one extra day of card-playing to his weekly schedule, continued with substitute teaching, and plastered community bulletin boards with ads for his woodworking service (these days the flyers, supplemented with color Clip Art, were coughed out of his former school's laser printer).

Dad found lots of things to do, including a scratch-built wooden deck for the backyard. He never actually threw away any of the junk in the house, but he bought large plastic containers to organize things in, and a daisy-wheel label maker to mark each bin. The entire inside of the house was a work-in-progress, without any real progress being made.

He decided he wanted a dog. "Your mother wouldn't let me have one after Atlas. Too much trouble. Too many germs." Several weekends, I went with him to PetSmart or the Humane Society, but he never quite found one to suit him. In the meantime, he built several prototype dog houses of different sizes. Each time I visited, it seemed like there was a new dog house in the back yard.

I counted four of them back there the day of his stroke.

• • •

"Dad?"

His television's volume was turned up, making me strain to hear him. He was using a speaker phone that came pre-installed in his new living room recliner. I knew something was wrong: I usually initiated our phone contact these days, to the point where I suspected he'd forgotten my home number.

"Nathan, where are you?"

"My apartment. Right where you called me."

"No, why aren't you here?"

Maybe he only wanted me to meet him for some project or another. Another futile shopping trip for a new dog. "We didn't make any plans, Dad."

"It's Saturday. Your mother's expecting you."

His speaker phone caught a sudden blare of music from the television. A woman's voice drifted under the music, and I told myself it didn't sound like Mom.

"I'll be right over, Dad."

● ● ●

Although Dad didn't scrub things spotless as Aunt Lora had, he followed her technique of clearing a path from one usable island to another. His bathroom, his side of the bed, one section of kitchen counter and one uncovered place setting at the table. The living room chair, and the woodworking station in his garage.

He was in the new recliner when I got there, and looked up at me with a surprised expression. The chair was gigantic, with thick arms and puffy cushions at the back, layered like rolls of fat. My father looked shrunken and weak in the new chair, his formerly stocky frame now thin after the removal of sugar from his diet. I wondered how he'd maneuvered the massive chair into the house.

He lifted an open package of sugar free caramels from the floor beside his chair. "Want some? Tastes just like the real thing."

I waved the package away and tried to speak gently. "Why'd you call me?"

"I didn't."

"You did." I pointed to the arm of his recliner. "The phone compartment's open."

"Oh. I don't really know how to work that darn thing yet."

Two blue plastic bins sat open on the couch, surrounded by newspapers. Tape labels stuck to each empty bin said NEWSPAPER. "You mentioned something about Mom."

He tilted his head as if he were thinking, then I heard the wet sound of him trying to unstick a piece of caramel from his upper plate. "Let me show you something out back."

Dad stood up, keeping his balance by gripping each arm of the chair. He started to head toward the kitchen, but his left foot seemed planted in the floor and he walked in a circle three times. Then he sat down again.

I pressed 911 on the speaker phone.

• • •

Dad tried to talk over me while I spoke to the dispatcher. "I'm fine," Dad said. "I could drive myself, or have my son take me. *If* I needed to come in." I cupped my hand over the disconnect switch, and Dad's finger tapped on my wrist a couple times as I repeated the address to the operator.

I certainly could have driven him myself, but I knew I wouldn't be able to convince him to get inside the car.

"I'll call them back and cancel it," he said after I hung up. His arms pulled close around his stomach. In the large chair, he looked like a child.

"Too late," I said.

While we waited for the ambulance, I stepped into the kitchen for a moment of solitude. I looked out the back door, counted the dog houses.

• • •

The elderly get prompt attention, even in a small-town emergency room. They hooked Dad up to an I.V. and a heart monitor right away. He fell asleep on the stretcher-bed, and I waited with him in the curtained-off area until the on-call doctor showed up.

"It looks like you've had a 'mini-stroke'," the doctor said. She looked mostly at me, but spoke loudly enough for my father to hear. "Probably nothing too serious, but we'll need to keep you overnight for more tests. Okay?"

I nodded.

• • •

When I drove back to the hospital the next morning, Dad was gone.

That is, he'd checked himself out the night before. As soon as I'd left, he called one of his poker buddies for a ride home.

He was back in the arm chair when I went to confront him.

"I was fine," he said. "I had a mini-stroke just like this last year."

"Last year? Why didn't you tell me? Or Mom?"

"Oh, I wasn't going to tell your mother. No need for her to worry."

• • •

I visited more frequently over the next few weeks. Dad was often lucid, but would sometimes drift into confusion. He'd pause over the kitchen counter, as if thinking about which cabinet he wanted to open. "Dad?" I'd say. "Dad?" No answer, but in a few minutes he'd be his usual stubborn self again. I tried to talk him into hiring a part-time nurse, but he said the house wasn't "ready," and argued he didn't need a nurse.

"Well, why don't you call a cleaning crew in here," I said. "Clear out some of this junk."

During a few of his confused episodes, I wondered what would happen if I started arguing back at him, saying every angry thing I ever wanted to say. After all, it wouldn't hurt his feelings: once he snapped back to normal, he'd already have forgotten what we talked about.

One afternoon as we sat at the kitchen table, he looked right at me and started to carry on a conversation with Pam. "Your brother doesn't understand," he said. "Nate thinks everything is so clear cut."

That's when I yelled back. "Pam's not here, Dad. I'm the one who stuck around. She left home because of you, because you let Mom sink into herself and almost drag the rest of us down with her. Pam's the one who blames you for Mom's death, not me."

Silence followed. He nudged his half-empty coffee cup and his eyes seemed to follow a gentle ripple in the dark liquid.

When he looked up, he was Dad again, as pleased as if I'd just arrived at the house.

"Hello, Nathan," he said. "Let's go in the garage. I've got a story to tell you."

• • •

Some of the junk near the wall was pushed against the tracks for the garage door, jamming the mechanism so the door stayed half-open. A few boxes and RubberMaid tubs had forced their way into the driveway since my last visit. A wedge of daylight stretched beneath the opening, filtered by slats of unfinished wood, a bookshelf without a back, and an upturned Formica table. It was bright enough that Dad didn't bother to pull the metal chain hanging from the uncovered light fixture in the ceiling.

And dark enough to set the mood for my father's final cautionary tale. Aside from a few stripes of light across his legs, Dad's figure seemed gray and muted. Although his voice had a slight old-man tremor, its volume commanded attention. We stood amid the workshop tools that formed the subject of his story, and at strategic moments, he would rattle a toolbox, or shake the metal frame of an upright buzz saw. The tight quarters of the junk-crowded garage pressed me to stand close to him: we were the same height, but as his story progressed, my father seemed to lengthen slightly, like a late-evening shadow.

The first storyteller of my childhood was back, and I listened.

• • •

Once there was a young boy [my father began] who grew up in a neighborhood much like this one. He lived in a modest-sized home, full of many memories. So many, that they pushed him into a smaller space, almost like life had forced him into a box.

His big house became as small as the apartment you live in now, Nathan.

This boy was critical of everyone around him, but that meant he had to be critical of himself, too. He didn't always like himself.

That might be why he had the accident, as if he'd subconsciously decided to punish himself.

He went to his father's garage, where he'd been warned not to play with the electric tools. He turned on the drill press and the disc sander, and they made loud buzzing and screeching noises. Then he placed a fresh blade in the jigsaw, perfect for making careful cuts in thin strips of wood—the same machine people use to make the precise, interlocking pieces of a jigsaw puzzle. He pressed the red power button, and the machine roared to life.

But he didn't have a thin strip of wood to cut. Instead, he pushed his left index finger against the blade. Cut the finger off before he'd even registered what happened.

The finger wiggled on the work surface of the jigsaw. It rolled on its side, and the knuckles curled—either from reflex, or from the vibration of the saw's motor. The finger seemed to beckon him closer to the saw, as if asking the boy to cut himself up some more.

His screams were drowned out by the hum of the jigsaw, the buzz of the drill press and the screech of the disc sander.

The boy was sorry for what happened; he hadn't intended for things to turn out this way. So he turned off the machines, cleaned up the garage, scrubbed away every trace. He wrapped the severed finger in a paper towel and brought it into the house. He hid it where nobody could find it.

Then he forgot where he'd put it.

Do you see the point of the story, Nathan? We all cut parts of ourselves away, but we never lose them. Things stay with us—souvenirs with memories attached. We can't always choose what to keep, what to throw away.

• • •

So ended my father's only attempt at allegory. At first the boy in the story was clearly intended to represent me, a veiled criticism of my safe, sheltered life, with the finger-chopping as a clumsy Freudian jab at my decision not to have children. Then the story seemed a general meditation on regret, as Pam might regret leaving her parents' home at 18, or as those parents might cling to bitter-sweet recollections of their other lost child, Jamie. According to the moral my father supplied, it was also the story of a man who, near the end of his days, tried to explain to his son why neither he nor his wife had been able to throw anything away, each object in the house a potential container for a hidden, forgotten, yet precious memory.

The story's logic didn't hold up under scrutiny, but it had its own grotesque persuasive power. I believed in it, exactly the way I'd believed in all my Dad's stories as a child.

His story complete, my father's head dropped slightly. He turned to walk inside, but then looked at me as if unsure where to go. "This way, Dad," I said, and pressed my hand gently against his shoulder to guide him into the house and back to his armchair.

• • •

"Pam. It's Nathan. I need you to come home again."

• • •

I was the airport shuttle for Pam and Aunt Lora. My aunt went to the Stoney Mill Inn, where she'd stayed seven months earlier, and Pam got the fold-out couch at my apartment. Sondra still hadn't come with her. "We broke up, I think," my sister informed me.

Dad's viewing drew a bigger crowd than Mom's had. A few former students showed up; several former and current teaching colleagues; a handful of his regular woodworking customers; the expanded circle of card players. About sixty in all.

As the on-site relative, I'd been responsible for most of the planning. Essentially, I followed the decisions he'd made for Mom: I used the same funeral home, the same priest, the same message on the prayer cards. Same style of casket, open during the viewing.

Some people I'd never met or barely knew came up to me and said what a good man my father was, told me he was proud of both his children.

Equally? Pam and I had fought on the drive over, since I didn't think she was doing her fair share of the necessary tasks. She refused to take any time off to help me get Dad's house in order. "I'm not stepping foot in that house again," Pam said. "I don't want anything. You can have it."

As if there were some great inheritance to be found. Aunt Lora remained silent most of that drive. She clearly realized the cleaning job was too big, even for her.

At some point during the viewing, both of my relatives had vanished from the main room. I knew where to find them: at the side entrance of the funeral parlor, smoking.

Without energy for argument, I simply chose the sanctuary of familiar company. "Hey," I said.

"Your father has, *had,* a lot of friends." Aunt Lora balanced a long cigarette from a hand twisted by arthritis. She rolled ashes neatly into the ash stand next to the four-paneled exit door, and tried not to flinch when Pam tapped her own ashes over the sidewalk.

I stood between them, hands in the pockets of my black wool trousers. "The last time I saw him, I yelled at him about Mom."

"When you're old, you're used to getting yelled at," Lora said. "People think we can't hear."

I smiled. "For a while, he thought he was talking to you, Pam. Looked right at me."

"Wifty," Pam said.

"There you go. In one of your father's ears, out the other."

"I guess. He told me one of his stories afterwards. Remember Pam? Like in the old days."

"Did you *believe* him?" It was a taunt, but Pam seemed good natured about it. She probably didn't feel like fighting anymore, either.

"God, he did that to me too when we were kids." Aunt Lora crossed her arms in front, cigarette balanced carefully, and mimed a shiver. "Used to scare the wits out of me."

"I miss the old days," I said, and my throat started to feel a little sore. "It's so funny to think about that house in Maryland. Our dumb dog, Atlas, with his rope wrapped around the tree. The Lieberman's swing set. And I miss my best friend, Aaron." Then I started crying. I couldn't yet manage tears over losing my Dad, but I cried anew about Aaron. I wondered where he was now. What would my life be like if we'd remained friends, if our family had stayed in the Maryland house?

Aunt Lora reached out to hug me. "That was a long time ago, Nathan."

Pam studied me for a moment, then nodded her sympathy. She tamped out her cigarette in the ash stand and went back inside.

PART THREE:
EXCAVATIONS

I began with the hallway bathroom, one of the few places my father had kept functional. I'd need to use the bathroom myself while I was working there, so it only made sense to clear that space first. Besides, there wasn't much thought involved in sorting through bathroom items. Most of it I could toss immediately into one of the thick green trash bags I'd bought in bulk from Sam's Club in Gadsden. A dozen or so toothbrushes, large packs of disposable razors, four different electric shavers (including one that looked like it ran from a wind-up key). Nail clippers and trimmer scissors (one shiny of each type, the others tarnished or rusty). Lots of prescription bottles, some of them with Mom's name on the labels.

The kitchen next, with a priority on perishable items. Each sweep through the chill refrigerator air mixed a new wave of odors: curdled milk, the sweet vinegar of spoiled ketchup, a yeasty tang of dried bread in an unsealed package. Why hadn't I noticed things had gotten this bad? The answer, of course, was that fresher items toward the front gave a veneer of clean; expirations dates got older the further back I reached, where spoiled items were packed so densely they practically created an air tight seal until I disturbed them.

Some of the items in the vegetable bins had liquefied. I held my breath as I pulled the clear bags from the bin and tossed their sloshing contents in the garbage. The last bag stuck to the bottom of the vegetable bin and burst when I tugged on it: orange and brown and green sludge poured out in chunks (baby carrots?), and a horrible stench rose up, a chilled bile I could taste when I swallowed.

I stepped back, ready to douse the whole bin with Clorox and Sunlight detergent. Then I stopped myself. Whoever bought the house would surely install a new refrigerator—new cabinets, new tile and wallpaper, and a new stove while they were at it—so why waste time? I held my nose, pulled out the whole bin, and dumped it into the Hefty bag. I twisted the bag closed, sealed it with the locking-tie, then walked it to the end of my father's long driveway.

After three hours work, I'd placed four bags on the curb for tomorrow's trash pickup.

As a break from the kitchen, I decided to go to Pam's room. My sister and I had made peace, but I still resented her refusal to help—it might be cathartic to toss some of her junk into Hefty bags.

The box of stuff Dad had gathered for Pam was still next to the doorway. Everything remained exactly as she'd left it, except I noticed Dad had removed the Jesus painting—the only sign he'd been back in this room since the day of Mom's funeral. I shook the box, retrieved my toy astronaut for a moment. On both arms, bendable wires had torn through the rubber elbows. I dropped him back in, then tossed the whole box into a new garbage bag.

The appliances were easy to throw away—out-of-date, with black tape wrapped around worn sections of the electrical cords. The storage box was another matter, constructed of impractical heavy wood that pressed a flat rectangle almost an inch deep into the carpet. I'd eventually need to hire some help for the furniture, especially the stuff Dad had made. Maybe a yard sale, but the idea seemed a bit morbid at this point.

Some of the cardboard boxes were surprisingly light, unopened UPS packages filled with Styrofoam peanuts and bubble wrap and some small item Mom probably forgot she'd ordered. I cut into one and dug through crumpled newsprint to find a plastic yellow fan the size of an alarm clock, battery operated and with a wrist strap. No date on the receipt, but the battery still worked.

After placing three full garbage bags in the hallway, I could slide one of the bookshelves aside and get part-way to the bed. In with some of the record albums and Book Club novels, I found old issues of *TV Guide* in the digest format, plus the grid guides from the *Washington Post*. Mom had circled some of the programs she wanted to watch, and of course she'd filled in the crossword puzzles in the back. I also found two volumes of Pam's high school yearbook, which I set aside in case she wanted them. A separate box contained a French textbook and a stack of different-colored pocket folders, subject names written atop the front in Pam's bubble letters, and bored doodles scratched beneath—hatched lines, cones, shaded spheres. Graded tests were in a loose pile at the bottom, along with a few English themes, handwritten on notebook paper. A theme on *The Scarlet Letter* earned Pam 75% and lots of red marks. I wondered if Pam had saved these things herself, or if she'd just given them to Mom.

• • •

As it headed into evening, I decided to take a break and give Pam a call. I dodged the hallway bags and stumbled toward the recliner in the living room. When I sat down, the over-cushioned chair was a welcome comfort after a long day of stooping and sitting cross-legged on tile or worn carpet. The phone compartment was already open. I leaned over and punched in Pam's number.

She didn't answer on the first ring. The thought occurred to me that Pam would notice Dad's name on her Caller ID screen, which might be like seeing a ghost—one of those old *Twilight Zone* episodes about a call from the grave. I thought about imitating Dad's voice, just to freak her out.

"Nathan?"

"Yeah." I leaned closer to the open arm of the chair and spoke into a small circle of dots beneath the number pad. "I'm at the house. First day of cleaning."

"How's it going?"

"A lot of unidentified objects in the fridge. I'll have eight huge bags of junk on the curb by the end of the night. Only about a million more to go."

"Wow."

"Hey, check this out." I moved my arm over the microphone, the tiny fan hanging by its strap from my wrist. I pressed the plastic switch.

"What is that? A bee's nest?"

"One of Mom's prizes from the Shopping Club. A plastic fan about three inches square. It puts out more noise than air, though."

"Glad you're having fun."

"You know I'm not."

An awkward pause. I switched off the fan.

"Listen, there's a lot of your stuff here. A whole box of tests and papers from high school."

"Damn, Nathan, I was probably stoned when I wrote those. Toss 'em."

"What about your yearbooks?"

"Got nowhere to put anything. Apartments are small in New York."

"Okay. If you're sure."

"Throw it all out. I'll never miss it."

I twisted the fan from my wrist. It felt odd not to hold a phone to my ear. Sound projected from a speaker in the phone compartment, but Pam's voice seemed to fill the air of the room.

"There's just so much stuff here," I said. "Most of it's junk, of course, and I don't want it. But I keep thinking, somebody else might."

"Yeah, right. That's the same logic Mom and Dad used to keep all that crap around in the first place. Don't fall into that trap."

"I guess."

"Set some kind of limit. Save one thing from each room, maybe. If it makes you feel better you can pick something out for me—just one, though. Your choice."

"Okay."

"It seems like—I don't know—you've come to terms with a lot of things lately. Don't get sucked back in."

"Yeah."

"If it gets to be too much, don't feel bad about throwing in the towel. Sell the place 'as is'—let the buyer deal with all the crap."

"All right. Thanks, Pam."

• • •

I found a half-dozen cans of Chef Boyardee mini ravioli in the kitchen cupboard, and opened one for my dinner. After that, I shifted to my old room for the rest of the evening. Just as much junk as in Pam's room, in no particular order at first, but as I plowed deeper into the room I found more items with a "Nathan" theme. Two boxes of my school stuff as well (in better condition, and with fewer red marks on the English themes). I also found a collection of old horror paperbacks and movie memorabilia—some of which I'd bought at a fan convention in College Park when I was in ninth grade. Lots of books by Robert Bloch and by the *Twilight Zone* writers: Serling, Matheson, Beaumont. Rolled-up posters and 8 x 11" stills from *King Kong,* and from Ray Harryhausen's dinosaur and Sinbad movies. I'd packed these away before I left for college—neatly, perhaps an early manifestation of a librarian's cataloging skills. They really might be worth something on eBay. Unless I decided to keep them.

I cleared off a corner of my bed and sat there to look at each item, returning it carefully to the box when I was through. I read a few short stories, paged eagerly through a "special effects" magazine and an issue of *Famous Monsters* with Chaney's "Phantom" on the cover. The evening got late without my realizing it: I'd lost myself in things I hadn't thought about in almost twenty-five years.

Many boxes still covered the bed, but I was able to balance most of them atop existing piles along the wall. Eventually I unearthed larger portions of a ridged tan blanket, and two pillows at the head of the bed. I patted the top pillow as forcefully as I dared, and was pleased that not too much dust flew out from the pillowcase. My mother hated dust and dirt and germs, but most of her life she was too tired to do anything about it. At that moment I knew how she felt: I stretched myself over the cleared sections of the blanket and allowed the back of my head to settle into the pillow. Beneath me the mattress was sunken and uneven; bedsprings creaked with each new shift in weight.

In the strange and familiar space of my childhood room, in the half-conscious moment before exhausted sleep, I lapsed into a childhood memory of prayer. Instead of looking to heaven, I cast weary eyes at a blank spot high on the opposite wall, where I imagined a framed portrait of a painted savior, still refusing to glow.

• • •

When I woke, I didn't remember where I was. The overhead light was on, but I'd set my glasses somewhere. I tried to bring my apartment into focus, but instead saw tall stacks of boxes that seemed ready to tumble onto me. My feet stretched off the edge of a wooden bed, its shape similar to the one from my childhood bedrooms, the Alabama and Maryland houses conflated in a fuzzy blur. I held a shoebox close to my body; apparently I'd grabbed at it in my sleep, then hugged it near my chin as if it were a stuffed animal.

The shoebox was sealed with string, tied in a bow. I held the box close to my face. Mom had scratched "Jamie" on one side with a ballpoint pen.

When I shook the box, it made an odd, hollow sound. I slid the string off one end without untying it, then flipped up the lid.

I recognized the colors first: red, yellow, green, blue, and orange. Two each, for a total of ten bowling pins. Beneath them was a pink, neatly folded blanket.

The bed's headboard had a thick flat ridge along the top. Without even thinking about it, I began to stack the pins in a neat line along the ridge, just as I'd stacked them on the edge of my little sister's crib.

The pins felt tiny, so frail I was afraid I'd squeeze them flat. When I moved them farther from my face, I couldn't see them clearly; my memory superimposed a crisper image over the blur of colors. There wasn't a bowling ball included in the shoebox, but Jamie never needed one.

I knew what to do.

I reached my hand next to the right-most pin, and swept through all ten in an even motion.

The sound of those thin hollow pins colliding together was like magic. In all the intervening years, I hadn't heard that distinct sound—it was packed away in a shoebox, muffled against the favorite blanket of an infant who'd died too soon. Now the past tumbled toward me with the tumbling pins. I was there again.

I could almost hear Jamie's laughter behind it all.

• • •

Then I heard a snap at the window, like a flat palm slapped against the glass.

Old houses can settle and resettle, the wood expanding from humidity then cracking back into place. During the day the sound goes unnoticed, smothered in the hum of appliances and ventilations systems and human activity; at night, after a disoriented waking, the sound can startle like a gunshot.

Followed by a scramble and slide, footsteps in dirt and fallen leaves?

Maybe I really had heard laughter earlier— but not Jamie's.

Graysonville was a small enough town; neighborhood kids up for a dare would know the house of a man who'd recently died. The same house that, for years maybe, inspired whispered rumors of an unseen presence, a strange woman who locked herself inside its walls. Late on a chill November night, a group of children might wander there, be drawn to a lighted bedroom then laugh and run as the bravest boy reached to rattle the window frame.

I stood up, my legs pinched in a thin wedge between the bed and stacked boxes. I felt along cardboard edges, and eventually found my glasses balanced where the lip of one box jutted next to the headboard. I pushed the glasses onto my face, bringing the world back into focus.

The bedrooms were on the shorter leg of the L-shaped house. The window of my old room looked out on an alley of grass and a line of trees that insulated us from the neighbors on that side. The footsteps, if they were footsteps, seemed to skirt the rim of the house in the direction of the back yard.

I edged out of the room. On my way to the kitchen, turning on lights as I went, I stopped to open the only item I brought with me: a tiny plastic briefcase I'd dropped just inside the front door. I retrieved the main flashlight element from the LightDriver kit and headed to the back of the house.

Sliding open the glass kitchen door, I stepped onto the raised deck. It wasn't my father's best job of woodworking: instead of removing the previous deck, he'd nailed fresh boards onto the old ones. The kitchen light cast my shadow in front of me; it stretched over the boards in an uneven accordion pattern. As I walked to the edge of the deck, a few of the boards seemed to roll beneath my feet.

The night was quiet. From the raised vantage of the deck, I squinted over the yard. Five of my father's prototype dog houses formed two rows in the back half of the property. They looked like monuments: grave markers for pets he'd never owned.

The smell of sawdust overpowered the scent of grass and tree bark. I turned on the flashlight and aimed its beam. Dark triangles wavered in the grass behind each pointed roof; carved door-less openings swallowed the light, the small interiors deep in shadow.

Five stairs led to the ground, and I made sure to grip the banister as I stepped down.

I swept the flashlight over the lawn. One large poplar tree loomed over a tool shed on the left side. Both of the shed's doors were open, with a riding lawn mower spanned across the entrance. Behind the mower, boxes of junk and newspaper were stacked too tightly in the shed to afford any hiding places for mischievous children.

I aimed the beam of light at my feet. Just listened.

Nothing.

I lifted the light towards the house, brushing a faint glow from the garage end to the living room. I moved to the corner window.

As I pressed my face near the glass, I recalled my mother's voice: *I don't want people looking in here.* The curtains were open, but a shoulder-high stack of boxes partly obscured my view beneath the raised shade. Storage bins and papers covered Mom's couch. I moved my head and a ripple in the glass shifted the room, like a dry wind had swept over the abandoned papers.

I opened my palm and slapped it flat against one square of the window. The sound echoed slightly. Was it the same sound I'd heard earlier when the frame of the house had settled—or when a young trespasser had tried to startle me? The noise seemed different out here.

After I pulled my hand back from the window, I fogged breath over the glass. A wet outline of my hand appeared, fingerprints and palm lines clearly visible. Then the water evaporated around the edges, shrinking the handprint so it resembled that of a child.

• • •

The night's chill air started to bother me. My jacket was still draped over one of the kitchen chairs. As I turned to go inside, the flashlight beam passed over the area beneath the back deck.

The deck was supported at each corner by thick posts. Numerous scraps of wood filled the space beneath—probably shaved edges and misfit pieces from long-completed projects. Strips of cloth were stuffed into gaps, worn clothing saved as dust rags for some hypothetical cleaning spree. I stepped closer and kneeled to examine Dad's handiwork. None of the scrap spilled over onto the yard—like a brick-layer, he had expertly packed in enough to fill available space, while still keeping most of the grass clear so he could steer his riding lawn mower over it.

Maybe it wasn't the strokes that killed Dad. He just ran out of places to put his stuff.

That's when I turned to look at the dog houses again. From my position lower to the ground, I could see the openings more clearly. It wasn't the angle of shadow that kept me from looking into each house. All five of them were stuffed to the brim with scraps and junk.

I moved to the back half of the yard, toward the two larger dog houses in the close row. More wood scraps and rags cluttered the first opening. I kicked at it with my shoe and none of the items shifted.

Plastic grocery bags filled the house on the right. The bags were puffy like balloons, tied shut with bow knots. A few of the loops stuck out from the pile. I shifted the flashlight to my left hand, grabbed one of the loops and yanked a bag free. It slid out easily, and the remaining pile of bags kept its shape around the small, deep gap.

When I untied the bag, I found several packages of sugar-free caramels. The candies seemed hard to the touch, and had no doubt gone stale. I pointed the flashlight in the hole I'd created in the pile and moved the light around, catching the glimmer of more loops of blue and white plastic, stenciled fragments of Wal-Mart and Winn Dixie logos. A faint chemical smell drifted from the gap. Probably, as with the refrigerator, things got worse as you went further back. To test my theory, I reached into the hole.

And something bit me.

I pulled back, brushing against another plastic bag, and the entire pile collapsed and tightened over my arm. Sharp edges clawed me through the shirt sleeve, and I felt more stings on my hand, palm, and fingers. Was it a bee's nest? My wrist was caught beneath one of the plastic loops, and the strap wouldn't break—it almost seemed to be pulling my arm in deeper. I panicked and tugged, but each movement brought more painful scratches to my hand and arm. Finally I wrenched my arm free, and several of the bags followed after it and tumbled onto the ground.

Pinpricks and drops of blood covered my hand, and several scratches began to bleed through from under my sleeve. I shone the flashlight on one of the fallen bags. Tiny metallic eyes glimmered back at me and stretched into metallic lines when I moved the flashlight.

Bags full of straight pins?

No. Hypodermics.

For Dad's insulin shots.

The chemical scent I'd noticed earlier now filled the air, a mix of rubbing alcohol and dried blood. Metal tips protruded from various places in the fallen bags. An entire syringe had fallen from the top of one bag, its needle an angry, gleaming stinger.

Dad was supposed to break off the tips and dispose of used needles in a red "hazardous waste" bin. Instead he'd tossed them into plastic grocery bags then jammed them into this toxic pile.

Why? He hadn't built these dog houses until after Mom died. Dad must have been more upset by her death than any of us realized. His inability to throw away useless things struck me then as a strange kind of tribute to Mom. Possibly he had also contracted her germ phobia: he'd moved the needles as far away from the house as he could, while still keeping them on his property.

Germs. God knows how long these needles had festered out here—long enough to rust and grow new bacteria. I might as well have injected poison into my arm.

The pain started to throb. My fear of needles surged up from my childhood, and I dreaded the idea that metal points may have broken off under my skin. I kicked at one of the bags in anger, then hurried back inside to rinse off the wounds.

• • •

I went straight to the kitchen faucet, turned on the water and pushed my hand into the stream. Initially the water ran light pink under my hand, but it soon ran clear. As the water grew slowly warmer, I pulled up my sleeve and moved my forearm back and forth under the stream, turning my wrist slowly with each pass. The temperature grew uncomfortable so I adjusted the faucet, but I wanted to keep the water as hot as I could endure—intending to scald away any possible infection.

After a healthy blush covered my hand and forearm, I turned off the water and examined the wounds. They didn't look as serious as I'd feared—small dots on the hand, a few tiny scratches near my wrist and one longer one atop my arm. To my relief, all the bleeding had stopped. And no sign, thank God, of broken needles beneath my skin.

I was angry at myself for getting in such a panic. And for doing something so stupid as to reach blindly into a darkened heap of trash. Then I was angry at Dad for placing those needles there to begin with—as if he'd deliberately set a trap for me. What was he thinking?

Finally my anger shifted to those hypothetical thrill-seeking trespassers. If they hadn't drawn me out of the house, I never would have hunted and poked through the back yard after dark. Of course, I hadn't found any kids out there, and probably imagined the whole thing to begin with—which brought my anger full circle, back to me.

Then a squeal of tires sounded from the road in front of the house, followed by a scrape of metal and a loud thump.

In that instant, I revised my theory of late-night pranksters. Instead of young children, I thought of teenagers, piled in a car and hooting at my parents' house as they drove by, maybe throwing a bottle or a beer can toward my car at the bottom of the driveway. I grabbed the flashlight (still switched on where I'd set it beside the sink), rushed to the front hall and pushed out the door. I jumped over the porch steps and hit the ground running. Night air brushed at my injured hand, cooling the faint burn as I raced over the lawn toward the road.

Not that I'd be able to fight a whole group of teenagers. The LightDriver had the heft of 2 "D"-cell batteries, but its cheap plastic casing would fall apart if I tried to use it as a club. Still, a rush of adrenalin drove me toward the curb, hunting for any property damage, ready to shake my fist at retreating taillights, yell threats at the vandals' car once the occupants were too far away to hear.

I stopped short of the concrete curb, at the end of the driveway. The road stretched empty in each direction, curving to the right at a distant "Slow" sign that drivers usually ignored. I could see a few neighboring houses, their porch lights dark. In the driveway, my Taurus wagon looked untouched, and there wasn't any damage to the mailbox (a popular target for teenage vandals).

But a rotten, musty smell hovered in the air.

The smell seemed to rise from the eight Hefty bags I'd lined up for tomorrow's trash pickup.

The green bags looked shiny and black in the dark, their only color from the yellow plastic ties locked around each closed top. I stepped down from the curb, and saw that one of the bags, third from the end next to the mailbox, was torn open in the side. Garbage and sludge had spilled part-way into the street.

Jesus. Just what I needed.

It was one of the kitchen bags. I saw the white corner of the vegetable bin from the refrigerator, the rancid carrot slop no doubt supplying the strongest of the odors. Zip-lock bags of other rotten food had sluiced onto the sidewalk. I had the morbid thought that these bags looked the size of kidneys or other internal organs, sliced from a person's side with a deep, jagged knife.

And it did look like the larger bag had been cut with a knife. Heavy duty bags won't tear easily, which is the reason they print warnings on the package: "Danger of Suffocation. These garbage bags are not toys. Keep them away from children and pets." A foot-long gash appeared in the side of bag, evenly parallel to the ground. The cut was too precise to have resulted from an accidental shifting of the bag's contents.

Well if it had been teenagers, they surely weren't happy with what they found. There's no incentive to slash open other plastic treasure bags after the first one spills out such foul-smelling garbage. The theory provided a good explanation for the squeal of tires I'd heard from inside. The teenagers drove away in a hurry: a peel out.

Leaving me to clean up the mess. It wouldn't be easy moving this stuff around, especially with a scratched up right hand and fears of new infection. I set the flashlight in the gutter portion of the curb, then lifted a Zip-lock bag by its corner with the fingertips of my left hand.

I was still freaked out after the nest of syringes, so I didn't want to reach too far into the open gap of the Hefty bag. Instead, I lowered each small bag into the torn gash, then poked gently with a finger to force it inside. The bags had an awful, sloshy consistency. It felt like I was poking at someone's stomach.

Once I'd finished, I briefly considered the idea of dragging all the bags back toward the house to prevent further mischief, then decided it was too much effort. Easier to simply get some packing tape from inside and return to patch the hole.

I bent down and retrieved the flashlight.

That's when I noticed the wedge-shaped chip where the street met the concrete gutter.

"Not too close, now, Nathan."

Cracks in the asphalt, and a missing chunk like someone had taken a bite out of the road. A niche to link with the interlocking tip of a child's tennis shoe.

An exact match to a visual aid from my past, the obstacle that tripped an unwary boy to his death in Dad's version of "The Big Street."

That image was burned so clearly into my childhood memory, and I'd swear this was the same shape. It wasn't a mark that would occur naturally, like a pothole that cracks and expands with the change in season. It formed more of a smooth, clean break—as if my father had cut it with some secret tool he'd kept all these years. Did he make this sign out of habit, as a territorial marking for any dangerous crossings near his home? Or through foresight, to have everything in place for future tellings of the story, ready to warn and delight the grandchildren he never had? Maybe he'd hidden this scary image in hopes I'd discover it, a kind of final farewell. He knew I loved his stories when I was little, and he'd never fully accepted that I'd grown up.

I placed my adult foot next to the curved niche, as if to follow that fictional boy in his foolhardy dash across the street. I thought of the sounds I'd heard while inside. The screech of tires on asphalt, followed by a scrape of metal.

Then a thump. Like a body hitting the road.

Was it possible, beneath the high-pitched squeal of tires…Was it possible I'd heard a child scream?

I could smell it now, stronger than the spoiled food from the opened garbage bag: the bitter, smoky reek of burnt rubber.

I aimed the flashlight over the road. No tire marks, that I could notice. But a stain of faded liquid darkened part of the street. The stain appeared at a familiar angle and distance from the niche near my foot. Years ago, my younger self observed the exact same shape in a road many miles away.

The outline of a boy.

My body shook at the thought, maybe a suppressed shiver from the November chill. I imagined an answering vibration from the street, the rumble of an approaching vehicle.

Nothing was there, in either direction, but I hesitated to step closer. The warning of my father's story held me back, just as his raised arm had once blocked my path into the road. I swept the flashlight's beam over the stain. Had my father painted it there, dripped oil to soak into the asphalt, outlining the shape I remembered: splayed legs, head twisted flat against the right shoulder?

A tremor went through me again, and the flashlight rattled in my hand. Its beam faded to a dim glow.

And the dark shape in the road started to move.

An arm first, unbending at the elbow then reaching up. Then the head, an inky smear that bubbled up over the flattened body. The other arm broke from the surface and swelled like a flexed muscle. Both arms pressed flat against the street, pulling the torso up with the faint wet sound of a scab peeled too early from a wound.

The shadow crawled forward on its hands, dragging the legs out of the road behind it.

Crawling toward me.

It paused about a body's length away. I stood there, transfixed and terrified. I could smell it: an awful mix of tar and burnt rubber, oil and blood.

Its head swung from one shoulder to the other with the click of a cracked neck, and it struggled to stand. The shadow's legs shifted, unsteady, and its arms swayed to maintain balance. Ripples flowed over its surface as it moved, a shaken mass of black gelatin.

When the motions settled, I tried to distinguish features in its face. Thick bubbles rose to the surface, hinting at the placement of an eye or nose, or popping with the sound of faintly parted lips.

Its right arm raised, a finger extended. It pointed at me.

Then the entire shadow burst, its image washing over me in a shower of black oil.

• • •

Heavy liquid poured over me. I tried to shake it off my hands, then pushed my fingers under my glasses to wipe syrupy blackness away from my eyes. An ashen sludge pressed against the corners of my mouth, threatening to force its way inside.

Dear God, what's happening?

Then it was completely gone.

No thick, smothering liquid. Only a light sheen of nervous sweat on my forehead and at the back of my neck.

I still held the flashlight in my right hand, its beam dim but resilient. My hand was pink from where I'd held it beneath the hot water; the small scratches and needle pricks looked clean.

Perhaps I'd had some weird reaction to the hypodermics. A hallucination.

The shape in the road...I passed the weak light over the shadowy outline. It was still there, but flat against the ground and less definite in shape. Unthreatening. Except I was still too afraid to step next to it in the road. And my right arm trembled so much that I'd gripped it with my left hand to keep the flashlight steady.

My scratched wrist itched beneath the cuff, and I pushed the sleeve further up my arm. Again I saw that pinched sunburnt look to the skin, held too long under hot water.

The wrist was white where I'd gripped it. The impression was smaller than my hand, though, like a child had grabbed and twisted the sensitive skin.

Enough. It's as if I was trying to work myself into another panic. My breaths came in heavy rasps, and I almost didn't trust my strength to carry me back inside the house. I sat down on the curb, a safe distance from the shape in the road and a few feet from the row of garbage bags. Rotten odors from the opened bag lingered strongest near the mailbox. The wind hung still, but drifts of the smell still carried to where I sat.

I cupped my left hand over my nose and mouth, and my breaths washed warm over my palm in heavy exhalations. The sound echoed deep and frantic, and I concentrated on slowing the breaths, softening the nervous tremors.

As I tried to calm myself, my breathing grew more irregular. A rattle and gurgle rose in my throat, then a strange flapping rasp added a new, desperate rhythm. To shut out the noise, I pinched my eyes tight and held my breath.

The flapping rasp continued over the expected silence.

A heavy weight shifted in the garbage bag closest to me.

• • •

The bag bulged at the center. I aimed the flashlight, casting a white spotlight with an irregular yellow center, like a firefly. The light transformed slick plastic into a curved mirror that reflected the curb and street and trees behind me, my face distorted and open-mouthed in surprise.

But it wasn't my face. A head was pressed against the bag from the inside. The fleshy tip of a nose strained against the bag, pushing the plastic outward in a small rounded cone. The flapping rasp scraped out from a taught oval stretched over the open mouth. Plastic whistled with each failed breath.

Someone inside the bag. Suffocating.

My reaction was instinctive. I didn't think, *How did that person get in there?* Or devise a vague yet plausible sequence of events: some conflation of my previously-imagined mischievous children and mean-spirited teenagers, with the older boys stuffing a kid from the first group in the bag and sealing it up, that child (yes, the head was small, like a child's, like—I didn't dare tell myself—the head of the awful threatening shadow that rose from the road just moments before), that child unconscious and unmoving until a terrified, gasping awakening.

My only thought: *I've got to get that kid out of there.* This was no hallucination: I saw a wrinkled forehead, brows raised in panic; saw the agonized expression of the child's open mouth, and could practically count the rows of teeth fighting against the stretched bag.

I leaned over the bag and fumbled with the plastic tie. The bag's opening was twisted into a firm rope, the locking tie pulled to its tightest available notch. I dropped the flashlight to the ground so I could use both hands, trying to curl the flat yellow wedges and thread them back through the tie's small opening. But the tie was designed to be much easier to seal than to remove, and I didn't have enough room to maneuver my fingers.

Desperate rasps urged me to act as the plastic swelled out then sucked in over the child's gasping mouth.

Break the seal. Let some air in.

I reached beneath the tie and grasped a loose fold of the bag. The plastic stretched as I pulled it apart with both hands, but it refused to break.

The bag remained rooted to the ground, heavy with the weight of the trapped child.

My knuckles whitened with tension, and the scratches on my right palm flared up in renewed pain. I tried to push my thumbs through the stretched fold, but the plastic wasn't taut enough beneath my nails.

More rustles and squeaking rasps of plastic over the child's mouth. My own breathing grew more desperate, my throat constricting in helpless sympathy. Time was running out.

Over the mouth. That's where the plastic was stretched to its limit. It might be taut enough.

I dropped to my knees, my hands finding the shape of the head and grasping it on each side to hold it steady. The texture of hair fluttered beneath my fingertips; an open jaw pressed against the heels of my palms. The child's face felt like skin instead of slick plastic.

Leaning close, I whispered towards one of the ears: "Don't be afraid. I'm trying to help."

And I plunged both thumbs into the taut area over the mouth.

The plastic stretched back, my thumbs warm as they passed over a wriggling tongue. The child's jaw tensed beneath my palms and I pushed my hands closer together to keep the joint from snapping shut. "Don't close your mouth," I whispered, afraid of being bitten—and also afraid my hands would press together too hard, crushing the child's head.

My thumbs pressed deeper. I held the head steady to keep it from pulling back.

Deeper.

Plastic stretched, and my thumbs hit a hard surface at the back of the child's throat.

The head shook beneath my hands in quick surges. Gag reflex.

Nowhere else to go, I pushed my thumbs together and pressed against the tongue, forcing my thumbs down the throat.

Deeper.

The head tried to shake some more. I held it steady, but the face felt brittle like an eggshell.

Deeper. The stretch of plastic.

Then a pop, and the shrill whistle of escaping air.

With it, an incredibly foul smell: musty and brackish, the scent of disease and death.

And, carried in the gasping expelled breath, a whisper.

A whisper of my name.

• • •

My hands pulled away, and I fell backward onto the lawn.

The bag shifted. The rattle of bones.

Then more of the bags shifted. More of the suck and release of stretched plastic over anxious mouths.

Faces pressed out from each of the bags, as if staring at me through a curtained window.

Too many to save.

Then a series of soft cracks, like the rude snap of chewing gun. Musty odor forced its way through tiny holes. Each bag acted as a bellows of foul air, squeezed to expel syllables over diseased vocal chords.

"Nathan," they called.

I pushed my hands over my ears and clamored back toward the house.

• • •

"What time is it?" Pam was too groggy to register anger, at least for the moment. Her voice drifted lazily from the speaker. I leaned forward and spoke into the recessed panel in the recliner's armrest.

"Late. I'm sorry."

Next I heard the rustle of bed sheets, a blind hand groping for the clock on the end table. "You're still at the house?"

"Yeah." A dim light shone from the hallway behind me. I'd lowered the living-room shades and closed the curtains. "Something's happened." I wasn't able to disguise the fear in my voice.

"What's wrong now?" A faint hint of impatience, or maybe disbelief—as if Pam already decided nothing more could go wrong. Even so, the familiarity of her voice offered comfort.

"I think Dad got worse after Mom died, worse than we'd realized. He kept even more stuff: newspapers, junk mail, spoiled food—with

brand-new storage bins he never bothered to fill
with anything. Instead, he stuffed wood scraps
and rags up under the back porch. And remember
those dog houses I told you about?"

"Sure."

"Five of them on that raised hill at the back
of the yard. All of them packed to the brim with
garbage. The biggest one was filled with a bunch
of those plastic grocery bags, tied shut at the
handles. I reached in and pulled one out, and
my hand and arm got all scratched. Several bags
were filled with hypodermic needles."

"Jeez."

"Like Mom's story about drug fiends in the
woods, back in Maryland. Except these were
from Dad's insulin shots. He used the needles,
bagged them up, then stored them in one of the
dog houses."

"More trouble than actually throwing things
out the normal way."

"Exactly. He had some odd reasons for what
he did, some weird logic."

"I've always thought that."

"No, Pam. Something more. At the funeral
home, I didn't mention all the details about
Dad's last story. It was about me as a boy, and
it was really gruesome. In the story, I cut off
my finger—on purpose, okay—then wrapped
it up in a box and hid it in the house. Dad was
disoriented before and after, but as he told the
story he was completely lucid. Like the old
days. He'd summoned the strength of mind for

a specific purpose, as if he needed to tell me this particular story. But the story didn't make any sense. Unless he was simply trying to creep me out—back then, and even now as I'm cleaning the house. I swear, Pam, it's like I spent the whole day half-expecting to discover severed body parts in a shoebox."

"You always put too much faith in Dad's stories."

"Listen. I came up with this analogy a while back. You know those invisible fence gadgets they sell for dog owners? The animal comes too close to a radio signal near the edge of the property, and it triggers an electric shock in the dog's collar. The stories were warnings to keep us in line, and that's how they worked for me. If I got too close to the Big Street, for instance, it's like something zapped me in the head. Reflex. Classic Pavlovian conditioning."

"Can we save the philosophy, or dog psychology or whatever? It's after four o'clock, and—"

"There's more," I said, my voice rising. I wanted to keep talking with my sister, and I knew I was avoiding the point, starting to ramble. But it would sound too crazy if I simply blurted out what I thought was happening: that for some unknown reason, my parents or their stories were haunting me; that I'd seen some kind of apparition, actually laid my hands on the face of a ghost. The trappings of psychology, an indirect approach through metaphor and analogy, gave plausibility and poetic truth to my account. "It's like Dad left traps here, or like some part of Mom stayed behind in the house she wouldn't leave while she was alive. Emotional triggers, maybe, like how those needles in the back yard reminded me of Mom's warnings about dope fiends. I got stuck by a few of those needles, Pam. The whole night started to get weird on me."

"What, you think you got drugged by something?"

"Maybe it was only the shock of reaching into a bag of needles. You know my phobia, and how I'd freak out about rust, tetanus, or dried blood. Then I thought I heard one of those kids out front."

"Kids?"

"That's what woke me up to start with. I'd fallen asleep in my old bedroom, and I heard a tap and some kid's laugh outside the window. The locals would have known Dad died, and Mom's spooky stay-at-home reputation might have drawn them to investigate the empty house. I was going to chase them down and surprise them."

"They woke you up?"

"Yeah."

"You're awake now, right?"

"Well, yeah." I'd paused briefly, as if I had to stop and think before answering. "Of course."

"Nathan, here's what you do. Get out of that house. Go back to your apartment, and take a break from the cleanup for a day or two."

"I will. I will." In the dimly lit room, I stared at the curtains I'd closed earlier. I hadn't wanted anyone to look in. "It's late, though. I'll wait until morning."

"Get help if you need it. With the cleanup or...with other things. You seemed pretty together at Dad's funeral, and it was nice to hear you'd come to terms with that mess from the past—you know, Aaron and the creek and all."

"I still think about it."

"I'm glad you remembered."

"Doesn't matter that we were only little kids. Things like that stay with you, Pam. It changed everything."

"Of course it did. Watching your best friend drown. Probably feeling responsible, like I did for—"

I gasped.

• • •

"Nathan? Oh God, Nathan, I thought you knew." Pam pleaded, as if afraid I wouldn't respond. "You mentioned him to Aunt Lora the day of Dad's funeral—how sad or sorry you were about Aaron. I really thought you'd remembered." Her words cracked in the speaker; they seemed to vibrate through the chair cushions on either side of my head. "I shouldn't have said anything."

"No, no. It's all right." My voice projected a clinical calm, probably far more ominous than the nervous tremor I'd displayed during my previous ramblings. "Tell me."

"I can't, Nathan. All these years we never discussed it. Not really."

"Because of me. You protected me."

"My little brother."

"That's why I gasped: I started to remember. To feel the truth. I can't explain right now, but I need you to tell me everything. I need you to tell me, Pam."

Because there was another reason why I gasped.

• • •

If you're sure, Pam said.

She began with the syringe Aaron had transformed into a squirt gun, the bait that lured us deep into the woods. Twisted paths, Aaron leading the way with goofy certainty. The downhill trudge, our discovery of the flooded creek. How they both made fun of my muddy clothes, and Aaron revealed he'd tricked us and hadn't actually found his needle in the woods.

(Yes, I thought to myself. Go on.)

How, in retaliation, I'd dared Aaron to climb the log that spanned the roaring stream.

(I've always admitted that part, and regretted it.)

Aaron slipped and fell in the water, and I laughed at him.

(No, I didn't laugh right away. Did I?)

Aaron was out of reach. We told him to swim, but the current was too strong in front of him. He tread water, hands cupped and arms waving.

(Yes. Like a mime in a windstorm.)

As for ourselves, neither Pam nor I had yet learned how to swim. She came up with the idea of a human chain, holding my arm to extend our reach from the water's edge. Aaron, tired and scared, liked the idea, but I'd refused to step close to the creek.

(The awful smell. But the water was also deeper than I remembered.)

Then Pam told me—if I was *certain* I wanted to hear more—Pam told me how I'd done this thing with a stick. A low-hanging branch I'd bent then ripped from a nearby tree. I held it out to Aaron, pushing it clumsily close to him, possibly interrupting the rhythm of his treading arms, slapping at the water and yelling "Grab it," but the four-foot branch too heavy in my grip, an out-of-control wobble and somehow the tip pressed against his shoulder, snagging the shirt. It almost looked like I intended to push Aaron under the water.

(I was trying to help.)

She told me how Aaron did go under, then flailed up for a second, caught in a current that gripped him from beneath to drag him away. "Swim," I had yelled. "Why don't you swim?" His body rushed down the creek. Aaron's arms flailed, and he dropped beneath the surface.

(No, that was a cardboard box. It caught a spin in the current, then sailed out of sight.)

Pam didn't mention a cardboard box. She told me how I'd yelled after Aaron, begged him to swim, then shifted to cursing—words she'd never heard me use before, angry wild shouts and name-calling and then more tearful pleas for him to swim.

(Oh. *I* had cursed at *him.*)

Long minutes passed beside the creek, each more breathless, more hopeless. Pam had reached out to hug me, but I shrugged away and ran back through the woods.

• • •

"Are you all right, Nathan? You've been pretty quiet."

"I'm just...processing." Despite deep layers of memories that conflicted with Pam's version of events, I knew she was telling me the truth. But so many pieces still didn't fit. It was like heavy lifting, my mind trying to shift and tug and force each new revelation into place. "When you caught up with me, Pam...you told me, 'He's right behind us'."

Silence for a moment. Then Pam said: "You asked me how Aaron would find his way out of the woods. It was like you'd already forgotten what happened. I guess I just wanted to calm you down, since you'd been so hysterical back at the creek. So, yeah—I told you Aaron was following us."

"I saw him."

"When you looked behind that first time, a wave of relief just washed over your face. I wasn't going to take that away from you. So I said it again and again as we ran toward home: 'He's right behind us. Keep going.' A couple times, your expression when you looked over your shoulder was so convincing. You almost made me believe my own lie."

I closed my eyes, trying to picture what happened next. "We went straight home," I said. "Mom called me into the living room and—"

"No," Pam interrupted. "I had to practically carry you inside. Mom yelled for Dad so loud he could hear her from the garage. We both looked awful, but you were warm with fever and nearly fainted."

"I remember being sick for a few days…"

"More like a week. We protected you from the search and recovery of Aaron's body, the investigation, Mom's long tearful phone calls with Mrs. Lieberman. I had to explain on my own how it was all an accident, how we did the best we could but weren't able to pull Aaron from the creek. It was so awful, Nathan. In the newspapers and everything. Nobody in the neighborhood would speak to me. I wanted to talk with you about it—to ease my mind I guess—but obviously couldn't. Dad went through a pretty tough time, too."

I stared at the curtains again, trying to trace patterns in the dark folds. "Wait," I said. "Wait. I saw Aaron later. At the swing set."

"One day while you were still sick, I walked in to check on you and your bed was empty. I never guessed you'd have the nerve to wander over to the Lieberman's back yard."

"David was there. And Aaron sat in one of the swings."

"The swing set was still broken when I arrived," Pam said. "I heard you yell. David had you on the ground and was pounding your back with his fists. I pulled you away, and David chased us to the end of their yard, warning us never to come back. The guy was always kind of a jerk— but he'd lost his little brother, you know?"

"It's like I can still see Aaron sitting there in the swing, staring at me. Angry and refusing to speak." Another revised memory shifted awkwardly into place. "I told David I'd tried to help Aaron out of the water, but he wouldn't believe me. So I looked right past him, and begged Aaron to speak the truth about what happened. That's when David threw the first punch."

Pam sighed, relieved to be near the end of the story, and also relieved she'd finally told it to me after all those years of silence. "The whole family had to move after that," she said. "Just packed up all that junk and moved, practically in the middle of the night. We had to, before we got chased out by an angry mob or something—like those frenzied, torch-waving townspeople who storm Dr. Frankenstein's castle."

I gave a quick laugh to acknowledge Pam's comparison. "I don't remember the move at all. It's like I suddenly appeared in a new house in Alabama. New house, but a lot like the old one."

"We protected you, Nathan. It seemed like the right thing to do."

"Maybe it was," I said.

Pause. "You think you'll be all right?" Pam asked. "I mean, it's a lot of stuff all at once."

"Yeah, I'll be okay. I really did need to hear everything. Thanks for telling me."

"Sure. Call me tomorrow, okay?"

"I will. Not so late next time, though—right?"

"Right. Good night."

"Good night, Pam. Bye."

My arm trembled as I reached over to click off the phone.

A lot of stuff all at once, indeed. I took a few deep breaths to brace myself.

"Hello, Aaron," I said.

Surrounded by the musty smell of the creek, amid the rustle of curtains and the crackle of dry newsprint, I heard my name again.

• • •

I'd gasped for two reasons when Pam revealed that Aaron had drowned. First, despite what I'd remembered for so many years, an instantaneous awareness that Pam spoke the truth. Second, the growing dread I was no longer alone in my parents' house.

It had been difficult to remain calm, to keep my sister talking so she'd tell me everything, everything, without worry that I'd fall apart. Her words reshaped my childhood memories, wrenched my past into new perspectives. As she spoke, an extra presence struggled into the room, breaking through into a world I'd always assumed I understood.

Until that point, my experiences that night had been terrifying, yet dream-like. An air of unreality separated me from the supernatural events: I was a spectator, simply waiting for the movie to end. I knew it would end, because there was no *reason* for it. My father and I had grown more distant, but children commonly aged away from one parent or another in their later years. There was no reason why he would lay traps for me as punishment, why he'd choose to haunt me though his stories simply because I loved him maybe a little less than I had as a boy. As for Mom, memories of her certainly lingered over every scrap of paper she'd written on, every item she'd hoarded around her couch in the living room. If ever a person's spirit could attach itself to a place, Mom's spirit could claim her favorite area in the house she'd always refused to leave. But if she haunted the house, she wouldn't haunt me. The two of us had grown closer towards the end of her life. We'd made peace.

The other possibility I'd considered was Jamie, her spirit summoned by the tumble of plastic bowling pins, her face pressed against the side of a plastic bag like the croup tent she'd pounded at with tiny fists in the hospital where she'd died. Again, though: no reason my baby sister would choose to haunt me.

But Aaron. Aaron had a reason.

As Pam spoke, I realized Aaron had borrowed the energy of the house, the crowded connotations of objects and sounds and smells from my childhood; he harnessed the residue of my grief and regret after the deaths of both my parents, inhabiting the evocative spell of their cautionary narratives.

The slap at the window, the scratch of needles, the rising shadow from the road and the faces pressed gasping against stretched plastic…All of these had been *attempts*.

Aaron wanted me to recognize him, to see his features in the bubbles of tar and blood and oil from the road, to remember his expression in the face I'd held and nearly crushed in my hands, the awful musty smell of the creek rushing from the punctured opening with the spirit's first attempt at speech.

But Aaron needed something more: my full awareness of what had actually happened that long-ago summer.

Not simply that I'd watched him die, but that I'd hatched some stupid plan with a stick that must have pushed him under the water. I'd cursed him for drowning, then ran away like a coward.

My best friend.

Near the end of my conversation with Pam, the shadows in the curtain formed a child's outline. Aaron's face appeared gradually, damp hair matted to his head, and skin the color of pencil lead smeared across a white page. He wore the familiar blue-striped shirt, now sullied with mud and algae. The apparition moved forward with uneasy steps, as if unable to connect with solid ground. Water dripped on the carpet. I wondered if Pam could hear the faint plashes over the phone line.

It stepped closer, one arm raised to point an accusing finger. Instead of a fingernail, a crusted scab pruned darkly over the tip. Skin on Aaron's face rippled with each shift through the air of the room; dark blotches of rot appeared on each cheek.

Aaron stopped when he reached the front of the chair—and I'd kept talking to my sister. When I laughed at her joke about an angry mob at Frankenstein's castle, I was afraid I'd *keep* laughing, a nervous tremor shaking my entire body. She told me the family had protected me, and I agreed it was for the best—even as the ghost of a dead child bent at the waist and brought his face within inches of my own.

Aaron's eyes were muddy and expressionless. His breath was a hot, rancid breeze.

With feigned calm, I agreed I'd call Pam again tomorrow. But to disconnect the phone, I needed to move my trembling arm close to Aaron's leaning form. I was terrified I'd brush against his chest: would I touch him, or would my arm pass through where he stood?

I thought I felt the weight of water droplets against my legs.

I greeted Aaron, and he whispered my name.

His small hand reached toward my face, and I could feel the scratch of a scabbed fingertip against my cheek.

EPILOGUE

Now, when I think back to that day at the creek, I wonder about my motives. Shouldn't my friendship have helped me overcome my aversion to the water? Could my momentary anger with Aaron have subconsciously influenced my clumsiness with the stick? Was it even remotely possible that I'd deliberately attempted to hurt my best friend? If so, what kind of person did that make me?

• • •

As I've mentioned, my sister and I used to hate those old haunted house movies without a real ghost, the cheap monster movies that never showed a monster.

In this story, Aaron is the real ghost. I'm the monster.

• • •

I sold Mom and Dad's house, eventually. Following Pam's advice, I stopped sorting through the junk and simply hired movers to haul everything away.

If the new tenants saw any signs of a ghost, I never heard about it. Nobody ran screaming back to the real estate office to demand a refund. No rumors of a haunted house arose in the neighborhood and followed me back to my apartment building.

Why would they? The ghost came away with me.

• • •

Do you see the point of the story, Nathan? We all cut parts of ourselves away, but we never lose them. Things stay with us—souvenirs with memories attached. We can't always choose what to keep, what to throw away.

• • •

Sometimes, I'll feel the stab of needles in my hands or feet, like the onset of arthritis—and perhaps that's all it is.

At night, I occasionally hear a squeal, crash, and thump from the direction of the small road in front of my building.

And Aaron. Aaron's with me a lot, offering me "toast" before I'm half awake each morning, inviting me for a walk in the woods.

That's the Aaron I prefer: the one who appears when I'm less inclined to blame myself for a few moments of weakness when I was only seven years old.

In less-forgiving moments the other Aaron reaches from the shadows, screams for me instead of my sister because I was his friend, screams across the years I'd forgotten him, denied the sights and sounds and smells of a living boy dragged beneath those awful murky waters.

The smell of that creek stays with me now. It follows me from room to room.

Through it all, another voice haunts me, my childhood voice blended with my present one, angry, resigned, heartbroken, as if life is something a friend would give up willingly or out of spite, as if I can once again erase my worst mistakes even while the truth pulls at me with the force of a rushing current: "Swim. Oh, why, *why* don't you swim?"